THIS IS FOR YOU

MICHAEL WILDING

Angus&Robertson
An imprint of HarperCollins*Publishers*

An Angus & Robertson Publication

Angus&Robertson, an imprint of
HarperCollins*Publishers*
25 Ryde Road, Pymble, Sydney, NSW 2073, Australia
31 View Road, Glenfield, Auckland 10, New Zealand
77-85 Fulham Palace Road, London W6 8JB, United Kingdom

First published in Australia in 1994

National Library of Australia
Cataloguing-in-Publication data:

Wilding, Michael, 1942–
   This is for you.

   ISBN 0 207 18425 9.

   I. Title.

A823.3

Cover image: Chris Barry
               'Dancing, Dancing, Dancing'
               From the series: Lost in Translation (1992)
Cover design: Liz Seymour
Printed in Australia by Griffin Paperbacks, Adelaide

8 7 6 5 4 3 2 1
97 96 95 94

For Jon Silkin and Lorna Tracy

Acknowledgments

Acknowledgment is made to the following publications in which these stories have appeared:

Antipodes, Aspect, Australian Book Review, The Australian Literary Quarterly in *The Weekend Australian, Australian Writing Now*, ed. Robert Adamson and Manfred Jurgensen, *Crimes for a Summer Christmas*, ed. Stephen Knight, *Critical Survey, The Good Tourist and The Laughing Cadaver*, ed. Michael Gifkins, *Hermes, Inprint, Island, Meanjin, Microstories*, ed. Rosemary Sorensen, *Most, Outrider, Overland, Panurge, Paris Transcontinental, Redoubt, Salt, Skoob Pacifica Anthology*, ed. C.Y. Loh and I.K. Ong, *Stand, Stet, Transgressions*, ed. Don Anderson, *Ulitarra*, and *Urban Fantasies*, ed. David King and Russell Blackford.

Contents

I Am Monarch
of All I Survey

We went to see the hippy king, living in the mountains. He was in exile from his kingdom, which had dissolved. Now he was like the Duke of Windsor or King Zog, in mufti.

We were not especially fond of the mountains. I lift up mine eyes unto the hills, from whence cometh my help. But that is to lift your eyes towards them, which is different from going up to them, let alone living in them. From the distance they were a calming blue, but to be in the source isn't necessarily the same experience as seeing it from a distance; and anyway, the rocks and gum leaves are not the source of the blue, no-one knows what the source of the blue is.

We got as far as Homebush where the slaughterhouses were and death lay like a miasma over flat paddocks and seeped across the roads and railway lines. That was where we realised we had forgotten to bring the address or the phone number, so we turned round and went back. And this in a petrol strike too.

He had dictated the directions on the phone.

'Have you got paper?'

'Yes.'

'Have you got a pencil?'

'I've got a pen.'

'Fine. That should do. Right. You go up the mountains to—'

And I inscribed, 'Go up the mountains to—'
'And the first turning after the shops—'
'First turning after the shops—'
'Right. You don't go down there.'
'Don't go down there.'
'Then you come to the second turning—'
'Second turning—'
'Don't go down there.'
'Don't go.'
'The third turning—'
'The third turning—'
It has to be the third turning.
'Don't go down there either.'
'Don't.'
'Then you come to—'
I hold off writing it down.

'That's the turn you take. You go along there to a crossroads. Disregard them. And then it becomes a dirt track, take no notice of that—'

It was like the ten commandments; thou shalt not, thou shalt not. Very Old Testament. And then Sara who was getting pissed with Sam while I took down the directions on the phone scribbled wiggly lines all down the map I'd created from the negations.

'We've already got the directions,' she said.

'This your wife? Lily?' he said.
'Yes. Well, we're not married, but—'
'But you live together?'
'Well, yes—'
'I'm just making sure of her name,' he says, 'not checking on your marital status.'
'Ah,' I say.

We go through the house onto the patio. It is a house with a patio.

We have met his wife as we go through the house. She keeps her own name. Now we meet a big bold blonde who stands on the patio like living sculpture. We are told her name but I don't catch it.

'She makes porno movies,' King Zig-Zag tell us. His wife stands by looking enigmatic.

Lily sits down with her back to the view. The view stretches across chasms to mountains. I sit and look at it. It is an impressive view if you like views. You can look at the view and not look at the people. Or you can look at the people and keep your back to the view. We don't seem to be able to do both, except jointly. Which means that one of us is always ignoring the people and one of us is always ignoring the view. I feel like one of those people who won't look people in the eye. I won't look people in the eye. Some things I cannot bear to see. I lift up my eyes to the hills for help.

'Do you make porno movies or do you act in them?' Lily asks.

'Oh, she acts in them,' says King Zig-Zag.

'I'll put the sausages on the barbecue,' says the Duchess of Windsor.

We are given wine in crystal goblets. I drink mine and then go and get a can of beer I brought and put in the fridge.

'I'm sick of drinking out of vegemite glasses,' says Lily. 'It's so nice to drink out of crystal goblets.'

I suck up the beer from its aluminium can. I have no commitment to aluminium cans, but I also have no commitment to crystal goblets.

Sam and Sara were going to arrive early but when we get there two hours late there is no sign of them. We decide not to wait for them before eating. The big bold blonde has a train to catch back to the city. So briefly flashed before us, so rapidly snatched away. Perhaps they had the orgy last night. The marinated flesh splutters on the barbecue. We gaze at the view.

'When I used to smoke a lot I would spend all day just gazing at the view.'

Now he doesn't smoke a lot. Now he doesn't smoke at all it seems. They pour out these wines from bottles. None of the cardboard and foil, cut-price, bulk-buy wine casks here. But I only notice this when it is pointed out later. I am looking at the view, getting used to the idea that there are no drugs. I wonder if Sam and Sara managed to score.

'I'd forgotten people still ate meat,' I say to Lily.

'That's because you never visit anyone,' she says.

Ah true, we are all in exile from our familiar places.

I think I eat a pork chop but try not to think about enjoying eating it.

'I dropped a trip,' says Sam, behind his hand, as we walk out to his car.

'Did you get any dope?'

'Yeah, yeah, don't panic, I got some good stuff, you'll really like it. But what happened was Bob'd got this acid and he gave me a trip and so we sort of got held up.'

'Where's the dope?'

'Relax,' he says, 'it's here somewhere, it's nice stuff.'

We walk back to the house.

'Anyway,' he says, apropos the trip, 'if anything happens, any weird stuff, just you and Lily leave, just go, we'll be all right.'

Sam shuffles out to the patio with his shirt-tail hanging loose and his Greek bag full of poems and books and panadol and serapax and antacids and a bottle of bourbon. He gives King Zig-Zag a copy of his new book. King Zig-Zag is stoking the barbecue and impaling pork chops and chicken breasts, he is preoccupied by the haute cuisine of the hills and Sam presses on his attention like a blowfly on marinated dead flesh. King Zig-Zag graciously accepts the book and puts it on a table. Sam stands with his cock-robin stance, shuffling his feet to get the toes exactly on a line and not going over it, lined up exactly for permission to speak, for the intensity of breaking through to impermeable inexplicable self-proclaimed authority.

The big bold blonde picks up the book.

'Ah, poetry,' she says.

'Would you like one?' says Sam.

'They're ten dollars,' says Sara.

'Would you like one?' says Sam. 'Would you prefer to buy one or be given one?'

The big bold blonde exudes all her honey golden charm.

'I'd prefer to be given one,' she says.

'Why?' says Sam. 'Why would you prefer to be given one?'

'Because it would mean more to me.'

'Then I'd have to fuck you,' says Sam.

She smiles.

She turns out to be American. She travels the world. She has been to Afghanistan, Ayers Rock, Bangkok, Nicaragua.

I roll a smoke. Nobody seems to have any dope but everybody smokes it. Sam writes an inscription in the book he is giving the American. The Duchess of Windsor is driving her to the station and sits in the car hooting the horn. Sam is in the throes of inspiration. He writes things and crosses them out, gets half way through a word and forgets it, the car horn keeps hooting, the American keeps telling Sam she has to hurry, and it only slows him down.

In the end she gets away to meet her contact in the city.

'That's what they do,' says Sam, 'they use these attractive girls, send them round the world.'

'Attractive,' says Sara.

We think of attractive girls sent round the world we have known.

King Zig-Zag reappears in his Marcel Proust t-shirt. We notice a collection of Ezra Pound's war-time broadcasts from Italy on the kitchen table as we are shown round the house, the renovations, the timberwork, the matting, the tiles.

'Specially for us,' says Sam. The literary touch. To remind us of what happens to writers who get involved in politics.

We walk round the grounds. It is not all his, theirs, the land to the horizon, but a lot of it is. Some was once laid out in terraces and fountains. It has a literary history, it belonged to someone or other, King Zig-Zag tells us.

'I think that's rather nice,' he says, 'a continuity.'

'The enemy,' says Sam.

Like Winston Churchill, King Zig-Zag has been building walls, dry-stone walls to hold back soil.

'It'll fall down,' I tell him. 'There's an art to dry-stone walling.' I do not tell him what the art is, how could I? All I can tell him is where it is lacking.

More fine wines are produced, more savouring of the crystal goblets.

'What they do now,' says Sam to Lily, 'what they do is at all these business things, if they want to get somebody to sign a deal, they serve special sorts of wine, or if they want them to freak out they serve them something else, or if they don't want the deal to go ahead they serve them something like a downer, they've got all these chemicals they use for making the wines, they've been doing it for centuries and now all the chemical companies and big business are into it, it's just like you get people pissed so they tell you things, well this is like that only more complex, that's all.'

'The other thing they do,' says Lily, 'is coat the glasses with some chemical, then everyone has the same wine but they make sure that certain people get certain glasses.'

'Mmmm,' says Sam quizzically, his lips a tight line, waving up and down like a French mime artist performing the line of beauty, 'mmmm.'

The Duchess of Windsor returns from the station. King Zig-Zag disappears into the bedroom and comes out in his Dostoevsky t-shirt. Now for the abyss.

We are herded into the company car and roar down a bush track between flashing gums and indecipherable expressionist horrors. Then we stop at a point beyond which even a company car cannot be taken.

'It's not far,' they tell us, coming across like rural hippies at our urban fear of walking.

The Duchess of Windsor carries the hamper with gateaux and champagne. We file along behind her, along these narrow ruts like sheep tracks, except there are no sheep, other than us.

Suddenly the ground drops away several thousand feet in front of us. About three feet in front of us. There is no warning of this horrific experience. One moment you are struggling along a bush track, head down, next there is just the abyss in front of you. We concede it is a splendid view.

'Shit,' says Sam.

You could have walked right over it and never seen the view. Except momentarily at something per something feet per second.

Then she wants us to climb out on some devil's promontory and perch there eating chocolate cake and drinking sour, fizzy wine. I stand well back. They laugh, they mock. I remain immovable. Sam reacts somewhat similarly except that he is far from immovable. He stumbles around, I can see him stumbling down the devil's promontory and bowling everyone ahead of him into the abyss. He stays well back but that's no good news for the people squatting between him and the abyss. I stay well behind Sam.

The gateaux are all right. They were bought in town; where we have just come from only a more expensive suburb. But my stomach is not into gateaux. The crows wheel around beneath our feet. Or their feet. I am not close enough to see the crows but I imagine they are wheeling around waiting there. I have been in a number of temptation scenes in my life, the high building number, up on the umpteenth floor of the Arts Council building and surveying the city beneath. But this time, on this precipice on the mountain, I cannot see what is being offered. Perhaps now we only get the sense experience, not the offer. This is less a temptation than a test, a threat; has King Zig-Zag read one of those reviews of my work that talks of recurrent images of vertigo, and ascribed them to my psyche rather than to the architecture of our times and too much TV? Like his car chase in the company car, these media images for instant excitement penetrate our consciousness, we believe they are our images, our perceptions, our lives. How much superman has the hippy king absorbed? But his feet are firmly planted on the ground, we can expect no jump from him.

Sam raises his hand. 'Can we go back now?'

If he has dropped a trip I can see that all this might be rather excruciating for him. It is for me and as far as I know I haven't. Not consciously.

The boughs bleed as the car brushes past them. The soil burns as the tyres spin. Oh no, don't say we have to get out and push. But we don't. Big motor, big tyres, vrrrm vrrrm. The earth could open and swallow us. But doesn't.

Then we are back in the house for chocolates and more fine wines and the dope now diminishing as I roll a few numbers to relax by. One, two, three. And the Duchess of Windsor tells us about her poetic leanings and then Sam demands a record player to play a record he's brought up in his bag but they haven't got a record player. 'I don't believe it, they haven't got a record player'. 'Well, we've got a record player but it's packed away'. 'Well unpack it,' says Sara, 'you're supposed to be the hippy king, how can you not have a record player?' Maybe they're into cassettes, cassettes in the car, cassettes beneath the pillow, headsets for jogging, etc. It is all getting shrill now, Lily is weeping in the kitchen for some hard-luck story the Duchess of Windsor is telling her, I sit in the armchair in the living room or whatever they call it here, the library, there are books around so maybe this is the library, Sara decides the Duchess of Windsor is making a line for me so comes and sits on my lap to protect Lily's interests, now the darkness has swirled round the house, chocolates and fine wines, and Sara insists Sam should read a poem, they've brought him up here they should sit and hear a poem, 'Here here,' says King Zig-Zag, remembering his cheer-leader days for the debating team, especially if there is no record player, 'I don't want to read I just want to hear this record,' says Sam, 'Read, damn you, read,' says Sara, so he reads, which means going into the preliminaries of setting the scene, the composition of place, a street at the Cross, Sam drunk and picked up by the pigs, more prison experiences, let me tell you my hard-luck story, the cell floor flowing in piss, 'This is real, damn you,' says Sara, 'this is what it's like being a poet.' 'Well, I can see it's difficult,' says King Zig-Zag, woof woof and other such woof-woofing, then the Duchess of Windsor reads a poem, from the collected works of Stevie Smith, against whom we have nothing personally, but it's all getting a bit like charades. 'Oh, I'm so frustrated,' Sara suddenly yells out, and the Duchess of Windsor suppresses a yawn and makes discreet intimations of retiring and King Zig-Zag starts talking about making tracks and one last cup of coffee for the road and Sam said he'd have the coffee but wasn't ready for the road just yet, it still being early in the evening, and besides he couldn't drive right now having dropped a trip. It didn't especially matter whether he had or hadn't, or if he had done eight hours earlier he should be down by now, and the fact that no-one had remarked anything till now showed clearly enough no-one would ever know the difference, but King Zig-Zag freaked and Sam had gained a delay. It went on for several hours. He was prised out of the house once or twice but usually scuttled back in or had other people scuttling back in for lost objects. In the end we did what he'd told me to do, just leave, and we just left them sitting in the car on the bush track, Sam and Sara, the lights coming on and off, the motor stopping and starting, and at some point Sam threw his Greek bag full of books and records and his scrapbooks into the abyss, but a bushwalker's mother phoned them up a couple of days later saying the scrapbooks had been found and did they want them back, which was good since he's just been able to sell them to the National Library for a few thousand dollars, since even poets of the most chameleon variety cannot live on air and the free lunches always turn out to have their price.

Outlines for
Urban Fantasies

We are in these modules with our notebooks, recorders, videos. We prefer these to external reality. We can get most of the books and tapes and discs and cassettes we want. We have quite sophisticated systems so we can make up our own tapes from the channels of the library. They come through the vacuum chute like all the deliveries we get. When I say we, there is an element of conjecture. I assume others are as I, that I am not alone, I am as they, we are more than one. Though the only one I know of is myself. Assuming I am myself; yes, I've been through that one, the dreamer dreamed, the figure in the carpet, the character of a novel, the hologram of a dream machine. I am no more especially a fictional artefact than are you, my hypothetical reader. I assume you exist reading this now and you are not an arrangement of lines on a screen, a minor character not wanted at the moment, a novelist's figment, an artificial intelligence machine scanning for the data bank, etc. So no more am I. Why should you think that? To reject what you fear? But to reject what I fear I have to believe in you, believe that there are others of us, locked away in our modules, world literature, art and movies at our finger tips, total music, finest quality heads on tap, turn the tap and kif, hashish, cocaine, whatever you punched into the keyboard pops out, all debited to your credit card account, don't need

to move to get it, safer than going out on the streets WHERE
GIANT FERAL DOGS RUN WILD AND BANDS OF BANDITS ROAM
AT WILL.

So we don't go out. Never visit. Never see no-one. No more
bars, no more lazy dives, the dust-laden air settles down on
the steps into the chiaroscuro room. The last card tables are
stacked against the wind, the umbrellas gone, the chairs
upside down on top of each other, the skeletal forms of
tourists locked in various sexual embraces and their flesh
pecked away by the vultures and the rats and ants, never
forget the ants, and their bones locked together till next
season and this was the last season.

> *who knows the plan*
> *of the ants*
>
> *people say they work too much*
> *i say they are playing games with us*
>
> *and their aims*
> *are beyond our politics*
>
> **RUDI KRAUSMANN**

So some places got very hot and some very cold, with this
ending of the seasons. Most of us were already underground
by then anyway. The tower colonies all got eaten away by
acid rain and killer wasps. These beautiful apartments, storey
upon storey in the sky rising from their narrow plot, bold
blazing windows facing across the bay, across the desert, and
their surfaces crumbling, the rain eroding their smooth
angular edges, the wasps building nests in their cracked
surfaces, excavating into the buildings. It all happened very

rapidly, so much acid rain, so many killer wasps, so rapidly they only recorded a few on video, these sudden spectacular internal collapses of the monoliths, the roar, the dust, the dislocated floors and walls and doors and windows falling, the broken ankles, the feet of clay, it had all been envisioned in the fragmented broken forms of the artists, now it was realised, their seismic sensitivities, their prophetic vision, even when they themselves asserted it was pure formalism, expressionism, never did they know it was all to be.

It cannot have been that their idea was the cause of the trouble, later to be realised in matter. Many claimed to believe this to purge and victimise and disappear those whose visions had been prophetic. These expounders of idealism, or their thinking manipulators, knew too well the falsity of that view, knew the falsity of their entire position. They knew the material base was truly replicated in those falling buildings. The artists had previsioned and such skills were not to go unpunished. So art was discredited, prophecy derided. You can still see the images in the video bank. A few have been wiped. Forgotten. Judged crude and dropped from the repertory. And the artists? I assume they are like the rest of us, in their modules, afraid to go out, taking advantage of total visual data bank and purportedly pure drugs.

At certain times bells ring, chimes, sirens, to remind us of available services, like the street cries of old England, the plangent electronic perpetuation of *Greensleeves* through the suburban afternoon, ice cream, or a brief peal or so, divine service, that was how the streets used to be. Car doors slamming, visitors, whistles of paper boys blowing past in the wind, roar of low-flying aircraft, sirens of ambulances and fire engines and police vehicles, the squeal of brakes, the steady swish and roar of traffic, the constant detonations of burglar alarms. So we believed then it wasn't safe to go out and here we are. Wherever we might be. Underground. Underwater. We might be moulded into some metallic structure like a giant pomander and be cannon-balling through space. Well, we are, I guess. But maybe just a few of us, out to colonise. Or maybe buried in reserve to be shot off sometime. Or forgotten. All the plots are available in print or video form. All the plots that survived. And you can get drugs to enhance any particular interpretation. Paranoia or total well-being, heightened consciousnesses all indistinguishable in the end, all accessible. That's it. You want a story, a plot, a narrative, an activity, something happening, how can there be when we live like this, now even our plots have been taken from us.

We are reservists in the industrial army of the proletarianised intellectuals. Each day we go in, no formal check in, no Bundy clock, our status exempts us from the mechanisms of the forced labour camps, no, we stroll in, reach a hand into our pigeon holes, the serried ranks before the doorkeeper's eyes, this argus-like octopus, take out our mail, this is the ritual of the mailroom, fondle it, handle it, sift through the white noise of minutes showered down from the crazed timekeeper, the second-hand catalogues, the remaindered lists, the offers for sale of sex surrogate supervision. There are no orders, no microdots, no baci, no fortune cookies, no message in the lipstick, just the argus-like octoped making up its thousand mouths while simulating its romance, Violet Trueheart sets our souls afire.

Urban fantasies. Yes, I would like a sixpack assorted sampler. I understand that these are outline proposals. For further development I must enter into the finance agreement. Once finance is secured, development of outline will proceed. (In practice financing of fantasies was achieved in only some twenty per cent of proposals. That was the official figure; the true figure may have been smaller, though even that may have been a fantasy figure.)

Plot, plot, they called. Plot, give us plot. Their hands scrabbling at the sides of the trucks coming into the terminal. The big dusty square. Dusty in dry weather, pitted, rutted with mud in wet weather. The camels kneeling down in one corner watching as they chewed.

'You give us setting and local colour but we want plot. Give us something to make our lives meaningful.'

But there was never any plot. The great sacks were handed down from the racks on top of the buses, the net released that held them safe up there, and as they were handed down with bags and cases they were eagerly felt, the blind hands covering the canvas bumps and bubbles. But there was never any plot. Some said it had all been cornered by the air force and was being held until the price went up even higher. Others said it had been shipped out to the U.S. of Antichrist, by their agencies. Others again said the harvests had failed, blight and damps and mildew destroying it, falling white and limp in the fields, covered with the white powder of mourning. And at the bus stations and rail terminals they called out, 'Plot, plot, restore the meaning to our lives, find a shape for our destinies, return us the design.'

Now we have been totally commoditised. Now we will only complete our dreams for cash. With no cash forthcoming, our futures abort. They remain perpetually terminated, like third world women shot up with some substance or other. But we have shot ourselves up, or invited the shot. Our dreams are not being kept down because their colour offends.

Our dreams are cash crops and we try to sell them. We have no other cash crops left, we have no land left to grow them on, we grow all that is left to us, our urban fantasies. And now if the cash is not forthcoming, we choose not to dream. That way we don't cause trouble to anybody, just rot on the pavements like giant balls of dung left by vanished dung beetles; or like great marooned turtle shells, the turtle flesh rotted and dried and flaked away inside these immemorially old urns. These the receptacles of undreamed dreams, unseen visions, unlived lives.

A spaceship and we suspect the captain has bailed out. Or whatever they do. We don't know what they do. Maybe he rematerialises here once in a while just to deceive us. The dead hand. Opening the porthole. From outside. Crawling up from the vine-cloning experiments below. And the punkas hang there silent, still, the punka wallahs all gone. We sit reading *Time* and *New Yorker* and the *Pyongyang Times*, frozen in this cedar capsule, AD 1924 but '34 here since it took so long to reach. Maybe he comes back by holograph. Hologram. The captain. So old he farts dust. Even the graffiti are no longer renewed, the contract lapsed like the service contract on the video terminal.

I met this old stone figure on the beach; he'd been coming to the beach for aeons now, locked into the cycle, from the days he had dreamed of being a dreammaker. There were no dreammakers by then. All these people wanted to be dreammakers, but the dreammakers had all been wasted. All that were left now were slots for fabricators. They built the huge images that could be seen from anywhere on the globe, satellite holograms surrounding the earth. They took over the images that had been found in the dream vaults. They shaved the last remaining dreamers' heads and plugged them in to the evacuation banks. They had reconstituted computer models of defunct dreamers, and stimulated the cortex to try to generate new images, but the results had never been made public.

'The people of that age were phrase slaves. The abjectness of their servitude is incomprehensible to us. There was a magic in words greater than the conjurer's art. So befuddled and chaotic were their minds that the utterance of a single word could negate the generalisations of a lifetime of serious research and thought. Such a word was the adjective Utopian. The mere utterance of it could damn any scheme, no matter how sanely conceived, of economic amelioration or regeneration. Vast populations grew frenzied over such phrases as "an honest dollar", and "a full dinner pail". The coinage of such phrases was considered strokes of genius.'

(Jack London)

He made his fortune on this contract work. Knowing without letting on what he knew. The appropriation of the political fable. But the necessity of its meaning nothing eroded the whole construct. Nobody really bothered to look at them. The holograms paraded day and night, the air waves were saturated, northern lights, fireworks, mirages, eclipses, son et lumière, sturm und drang. They were hollow globes and no-one entered them.

The dreamworkers had been killed off but they might always return. No-one really knew whether it mightn't be an atavism, a recessive gene, a hope eternal, an ineradicable random generation. So they kept spores in case they needed to eliminate some random atavistic generation. And they escaped up the air conditioning vents and the director cut his throat on hologram satellite live transmission and the skies dripped with blood for twenty minutes of instant hara-kiri.

He'd been a good fabricator. He could have been a dreamer but no-one believed that there were any dreams left, only the ignorant believed there could still be dreamers. The spores spread but he assured them there was no plague. It comes from watching TV. The campaign worked. Deprived of controlled dream substitutes when the TV went they all ate tinned snoop and caught the terrible wasting disease. Many died, some survived but fixed at that moment of the catastrophe, when the international holograms all imploded and the spores spread through the tinned snoop, destined to cycle round and round and round like dreams that failed of a vision.

And the smoke filed along the salmon sand and the silver and azure sky and the reptilian tracks of the buggies spread into the sunset.

Not realising how far out he was, out in space there, weightless, floating in those great padded astronaut suits, like divers, like dirigibles, like Elvis in the last clips, and what was it, fifteen chemical substances in his bloodstream, so that blown up silicone look to the image, the visual correlative of all the substances and the developed hide-like ostriches' calluses, and down on the pavement the hologram of how he used to seem, only remotely connected with that free floating image out in space, only remotely connected with anything, either of them, hologram, space projection, figure, unapproachable.

Nobody really liked going near the mind prison. It had that contaminated aura, like the environs of the morgue or the courts, hospitals or police stations or the slaughteryards. You had to invoke protection even to write about it. Even then it still seemed a risk. One speculation was that some of the minds had somehow escaped and would invade your aura if you went nearby, let alone visited. And then they would lie dormant till you left and they would've smuggled themselves away with you. Others said this was impossible, no minds could escape, that there were no living minds there. They were not so much dead as benign, was how others explained it. Bombarded with radioactivity they would start off again. Or whatever else they did. Blow nicotine over them. But this only happened in carefully controlled laboratory environments. There were no viable minds actually alive in the atmosphere there. Lurking in the corridors and tunnels. Hiding out in the great vases. Clutching on to the carefully restored gargoyles on the old buildings. As soon as you entered the grounds all the symptoms of entity invasion developed, the headaches, the eyestrains, tensions, lack of breath. A lot of the regular service workers carried ventilating sprays for their lungs; or dosed themselves with prescribed antidotes before entering. Prescribed for what? We could never get satisfactory answers for that. Prescribed for tension, maintenance doses. Nor did we know how many were under medication. Observations suggested a high percentage.

The grounds were full of trees. Beautiful would've been the official description if there'd been a brochure. But great flying foxes and dusty moths lurked beneath those huge canopies, so it made us suspect other things hung there upside down, waiting for the bared neck to drop on; and this fear gave it all a deserted, paralysed air, the presence of fear manifested by these clouds of desertedness that blew through the grounds like tumbleweed in another metaphoric realisation. We didn't have tumbleweed here. Just fear. And the animal cries of the golden ones down at the arenas, great walls of sound, that only further agonised the feral minds lurking there, and there was everywhere, where they lurked.

One theory was that they didn't try to escape but just lurked there, welcomed the escape from impossible families and desperate domesticities; and since there was no war quite ready yet, not one they could externalise all their rage and frustration into, they found the mind prison an acceptable substitute, like a military graveyard, that air of achieved desolation. And the pain you felt visiting there or passing the environs was just these escaped yet still imprisoned minds sucking sustenance from you as you passed. They weren't trying to stowaway with you and escape, where would they escape to, but merely lit upon you as you passed, like fleas in a long-deserted house, or lice on the locks of literature. They liked their prison. And it was this that made it so terrible a place to pass by.

And others again theorised that there were no escapees, they were all willing inmates who liked it there, and further it was structured for them to suck the energies off the living who visited there, or the young people who were drafted there, and in that act of sucking infect the bloodstream, or vital ether, with the diseases of their own terminated condition. And this infecting, some theorised, was no accidental, unfortunate side effect of the institution and its parasitic inmate caste, but the intention all along. The inmates may have believed that the whole cycle was devised for them, for their support; never realising they were just instrumental in this social plan of infection. And them but the dirty needles who were never meant to be clean, or their hands. And it was this, not any hypothetical feral minds, that caused those intense sensations of sickness, discomfort, pain and fear in the environs and on the grounds of the mind prison.

And then a man came down the barrel of a gun with a door in his hands, which he shut.

Kayf

onderful was the contrast between the steamer and that villa on the Mahmudiyah canal! Startling the sudden change from presto to adagio life! In thirteen days we had passed from the clammy grey fog, that atmosphere of industry which kept us at anchor off the Isle of Wight, through the loveliest air of the Inland Sea, whose sparkling blue and purple haze spread charms even on North Africa's beldame features, and now we are sitting silent and still, listening to the monotonous melody of the East—the soft night-breeze wandering through the starlit skies and tufted trees, with a voice of melancholy meaning.

And this is the Arab's 'kayf'. The savouring of animal existence; the passive enjoyment of mere sense; the pleasant languor, the dreamy tranquillity, the airy castle-building, which in Asia stand in lieu of the vigorous, intensive, passionate life of Europe. It is the result of a lively, impressible, excitable nature, and exquisite sensibility of nerve; it argues a facility for voluptuousness unknown to northern regions, where happiness is placed in the exertion of mental and physical powers; where Ernst ist das Leben; where niggard earth commands ceaseless sweat of face, and damp chill air demands perpetual excitement, exercise, or change, or adventure, or dissipation, for want of something better. In the East, man wants but rest and shade: upon the banks of a bubbling stream, or under the cool shelter of a perfumed tree, he is perfectly happy,

smoking a pipe, or sipping a cup of coffee, or drinking a glass of
sherbert, but above all things deranging body and mind as little
as possible; the trouble of conversations, the displeasures of
memory, and the vanity of thought being the most unpleasant
interruptions to his kayf. *No wonder that 'kayf' is a word*
untranslatable in our mother tongue.

In a coarser sense 'kayf' is applied to all manner of
intoxication. Sonnini is not wrong when he says, 'the Arabs
give the name of Kayf to the voluptuous relaxation, the delicious
stupor, produced by the smoking of hemp.'

RICHARD BURTON, 1855

North Africa. Somewhere warm, somewhere to get stoned
away from cold weather and cold wars, somewhere to relax.
The need to relax producing its own tensions, of course, the
desire to relax, the will to relax, maybe not a need, put like
that Marcus would have hesitated about need, he felt guilty
about having needs, needing to relax being no need. But it
would be nice, and to obliterate all those anxieties about
unnecessary needs the sooner he could score the better, and
how do you score in a strange place where you know no-one,
don't know how legal or illegal it is anyway, is this the sort
of hotel you can ask the desk clerk, what about asking the
taxi driver on the way from the airport, is that insanity or
practical common sense?

And outside the palm trees along the boulevard and then
the railway line and then the beach, and first thing in the
morning boys playing football on it, just like *L'Étranger*, the
long stretching beach, the boys playing football and doing
headstands and cartwheels, the port at one end and the old
town above it, the new tourist hotels stretching along to the
other end of the beach, cargo ships and hydrofoil ferries
coming in to dock.

They went out of the hotel in search of somewhere to eat

breakfast, first one direction, then back and towards the port and the old town. A figure in black homed in on them.

'Good morning, how you like it here?'

Black jeans, black t-shirt, walking along with them but a couple of paces ahead and to one side, like a fighter plane escorting an alien invader of airspace.

'You from England, London, I have a brother in London, I like to practise my English.'

They walked along.

'I'm not a guide,' he assured them.

'What's this?' said Lydia. 'What have we got ourselves into?'

Marcus shrugged. 'I don't know.'

'Is he police?'

'I don't know.'

They walked along the boulevard, past the souvenir shops and the cafés. There didn't seem to be anything that they wanted to eat; people either drinking tea or coffee, or grilling meat. Marcus scrutinised them as he passed. One old man with a smiling, wizened face held a pipe in one hand and shook a round tobacco tin. The knowing smile suggested kif. Was shaking the tin a selling gesture, how would you know, and what if it wasn't?

'These places too expensive,' Mustapha said, he'd already given them his name, elicited theirs, the shops draped with blankets, rugs, windows full of brassware, leatherware, the smell of freshly tanned leather thick and yellow and sweet across the pavements.

'What do we do?' said Lydia.

Marcus shrugged, smiled, his smile tighter, less persuasive, harder to maintain now, the facial muscles tired, unconvinced. He didn't know what you did, he just drifted along, looking for some likely eating place, dope place.

'If it isn't him it'll be somebody else,' he said.

Mustapha walked ahead, keeping up a brisk pace.

'These were the cannon used against the Spanish,' he told them.

They were in the Medina, the tiny narrow streets and alleys, the archways, children helping weave, taking threads down the length of the alley, this criss-cross of threads, and the cross-legged tailors weaving, sewing, people calling from shops, 'Buy something from me', 'Don't trust the black man, he gets a commission from all the shops.'

At least if that's what it was about, the financial basis was clear, Marcus figured. They wouldn't need to work out a tip for having been shown round where they didn't want to be shown.

They came up to the casbah, a coach load of tourists watching the snake charmers. Marcus took one look at the swaying, hooded snakes, metallic grey, scaly dragon tails, that was enough. They walked to the walls to look across at the sea, the houses along the cliff. But what he wanted was something to eat, something to drink, something to smoke.

They went back down through the narrow alleys, the people with things to sell calling out from doorways, the others looking at them, this silent looking, the familiar passive watchfulness, blank doorways opening and closing directly onto the narrow pathways.

'Tell him we want to get something to eat,' said Lydia.

'You try,' said Marcus, surrendering to the flow of it, not knowing where or why they were wandering through this ancient alien city, so other, it was all so impermeably other, familiar from movies and books, but familiar only in its otherness.

'Here is the house of the lady who had seven husbands,' said Mustapha. 'You thirsty? We'll have some mint tea, I'll take you to my relatives.'

And on they wound.

They came into a shop that opened into room after room, draped with carpets, blankets, djellabas, kaftans, shirts, handbags, cases, little stuffed model camels. They sat down and drank mint tea and looked at all these things. Marcus tried on a djellaba and a fez.

'Now you look like an official guide,' they said, there seemed to be two or maybe three people showing them things, 'You buy one of these and you'll have no trouble, everyone will know you've bought something and they won't ask you any more, you wear a djellaba and you don't look like a tourist.'

Marcus doubted it.

'You're not wearing a djellaba,' Lydia said.

'Some days I do,' the man said, 'but today . . .'

A sad smile, no meaning.

Marcus found some hookahs and waterpipes in a corner and gazed at them with longing.

'You want one of those?'

'They're very nice,' said Marcus; 'what I'd rather have is something to smoke in them.'

'No, we don't smoke,' said the man in the shop.

'But people do?'

'People do?'

'People do smoke? Here? In the town?'

'Oh yes, people do, they smoke in the cafés, no problems, sometimes the police come along and they confiscate their kif and their pipes. So they go and buy another pipe.'

Marcus saw an endless vista of smoky, dark cafés, sniffing around hopefully for the familiar smell, for somebody selling, surrendering pipe after pipe to the invading police. There had to be a better way.

'Where do you get it? In the cafés?'

'In the cafés, yes,' the man said. And then he caught the drift of Marcus' laboured conversation. 'Ah,' he said, 'you want some? We don't have any, I don't smoke. But I'll send the boy.'

'Sure,' said Marcus.

Then he sat around trying on djellabas and sipping mint tea while Mustapha went off to score.

'He won't be long. You smoked before, no?'

'Yes,' said Marcus.

'You like it?'

'Yes, he likes it,' said Lydia.

'Ah,' said the man, 'I smoke a lot. But not while I'm working. Good stuff.'

'Good stuff,' agreed Marcus.

Mustapha came back without success.

'No good stuff in the casbah,' he said. 'We take a car ride. I take you to my place, smoke some good stuff, you know it's good there.'

It seemed fair enough. The terror of the unknown but a better price and a better quality out of the tourist area. Marcus bought his djellaba, maybe it would be insurance against the wrong sort of car ride, when was he ever going to wear a djellaba? It seemed a lot of money for a djellaba, for anything that he wasn't really likely to wear, but if the dope was cheap and you added the cost of it onto the dope and treated it as the necessary way to score, then you could write off the cost that way.

Back through the narrow alleys, finally they passed a cake shop near the Socco and stopped to stave off their hunger and then Mustapha hailed a taxi and they were going through the newer town, the colonial development, the new housing blocks. The Spanish mosque. The new mosque. The American school.

They stopped at a café, an open street, looking across at new housing blocks. The juke box or cassette player was playing modern black American music, commercialised energy, electronic precision. They ordered mint tea again and sat out at a table on the street.

'You wait here,' Mustapha said. 'Five minutes, ten minutes.'

When he came back they went inside. There were two rooms, the one with the counter, the other a bare room at one side. They sat there, out of sight of the shopkeeper, who brought them an ashtray and then went away. Mustapha produced a block of blond hash.

'You have an American cigarette?'

'No,' said Marcus, 'I'll get some . . .'

'No, I have one,' said Mustapha, breaking one open. Milder than the local tobacco, he explained. He crumbled a piece off the block of hash, crumbs lay on the laminex table top, he broke big crumbs of hash into the joint, Marcus watched transfixed, stoned already, imagine being able to use that much hash in one joint, what a life, happiness began to spread around him, Mustapha passed him the joint, lit it for him, and then the café was a sandy ochre, a soft capsule of warm, vibrating well-being, now they had arrived, now they could relax. He passed the joint to Mustapha.

He shook his head. 'No, I don't smoke, makes me too paranoid, you know.'

'Go on,' said Lydia.

He took a couple of tokes to be sociable. Then he produced the rest of the block from his sock.

'Two twenty dirhams, twenty pounds. How much would this cost where you come from?'

'Don't tell him,' said Lydia.

Marcus beamed. He had been trying to work it out, was it three times as cheap here, ten times as cheap, the bare white café room waved in the viscous gentle air, the whole breathing movement of the earth passed through it, nothing still, nothing solid, no fixed straight lines, but a gentle waving in the soft susurrus of the perceived day.

'What about the stuff you eat?' said Marcus. Dawamesc back in the Parisian 1840s, but the word, or their pronunciation, meant nothing to Mustapha.

27

'Like a sweet,' Marcus tried.

'Ah, majouna, you want to try some majouna?'

'Can you get it?'

'Yes, I can get it. Not now. But tonight. You want some?'

'Sure,' they said.

'You want me to get you some?'

'Yes,' said Lydia.

'You tell me your hotel room and I will come.'

The paranoia there, wavering, but there didn't seem any great reason not to since he'd already elicited the name of the hotel, so if it was a police set up they already knew enough.

'You'll be there tonight, seven o'clock, seven thirty? I'll bring it then.'

They agreed.

'We go now?'

And that was good, he'd made the deal, no more hanging around, as long as he would find them a taxi and they could get back to the hotel and have a relaxing smoke . . .

'If anybody asks,' he said, 'say you don't smoke. Don't trust anybody. Roll it in your hotel room and then smoke on the beach.'

'But not in the hotel room?'

'Yes, that's what I'm telling you, it's all right in the hotel, you smoke in your room, no-one bothers, if anyone asks, say you don't smoke. You don't look like you smoke, that's why I didn't ask you before. You'll be all right.'

They walked down from the café, down the dusty road to the market below, they waited there for a cab, rectangular buildings, women in kaftans, their faces covered to the eyes, men in djellabas, others in Western clothes, the rest just a blur, a warm golden glow.

They went out later in the afternoon, somewhat uncertainly down the stairs, past the burnished brass trays and pots, smiling at the smiling desk clerk, out into the bright light and the shadow of the palm trees. Marcus had never possessed such a store of hash, the future days were assured, the weight of anxiety slipped away into retreat, for a few days it was driven off by the soft yellow golden blocks.

'Hello, how are you?'

A figure in a black t-shirt and black jeans slid across from somewhere and was walking along with them.

Marcus nodded.

'Casbah, Bedouin markets, Medina.'

'We've already been,' said Marcus.

They kept walking and he kept pace with them, smiling.

'This you first time here?'

Marcus agreed.

'Where you from? London?'

'Tell him we already have a friend,' said Lydia.

'You tell him.'

'We already have a friend who's showed us round.'

'You have? That's good. You want to get high?'

'I already am,' said Marcus.

'Ah,' the boy in black smiled, 'have a good time.'

He dropped back and curved round to wherever he'd appeared from.

The palm trees swayed a bit.

'You needn't have worried about scoring,' said Lydia.

He thought about the djellaba. Maybe he should have put it on. Then they mightn't have been approached. But then they mightn't have found out how easy in fact it was to score. And even with that hefty stash for the future, it was good to know you only had to walk along the boulevard to score again.

'Chocolat, hachisch,' a voice called out to them.

The weights lifted from Marcus's already lightened shoulders. Even if he made a pig of himself and smoked it all he could always get more. Without having to buy another djellaba. After a while they turned round and walked back along the boulevard to the hotel. They waved to the boy in black. He waved. They smiled at the smiling desk clerk who smiled back. They climbed the stairs past the burnished brass, looked into the lounge in which they never saw anyone sitting, and then they were back in the room and Marcus could set about making a pig of himself.

They ate dinner in the hotel. It seemed easier than going out.

'If someone comes for us, we're in the restaurant,' they told the desk clerk.

But when Mustapha did arrive with his brother the waiter clearly didn't like it. There was a place for street hustlers and a place for tourists. A chill came over his genial manner. Mustapha and his brother rode it through. The familiar discriminations, the assessments and judgements and dismissals that permeate everything.

They hadn't got the majouna.

'Tomorrow. Tomorrow we will come for you and you come out to our place. You must meet our mother. You must have a meal with us.'

They were both in black, black jeans, black t-shirts, Mustapha had a casual black jacket.

Marcus ordered beers, suffering the icy chill of the waiter; once he'd gone the warmth returned, the table melted a little softer, flowed round, congealed against the outer influences.

'My brother is a law student,' said Mustapha.

'That way I can help my family and make money,' the brother said.

'What does your father do?' Lydia asked.

'He's a customs officer,' Mustapha said.

Lydia made an involuntary noise reserved for police, customs officers.

'No,' said the law student, 'he's a good man, a good father.'

'That's good,' said Lydia, she liked the idea of good men, good fathers, affectionate families.

'He is a good father. You know, like the movie. You know the movie.'

Marcus shook his head. Good fathers were rather out of fashion in the movies he ever saw.

'The Goodfather, you must know the movie, our father is like the good father, he looks after his family, anybody in trouble he looks after them.'

'The Goodfather,' said Mustapha, 'you know, Marlon Brando.'

'Ah, yes,' said Marcus.

The law student raved on. That was his ideal of the good man, the good father. 'I want to be a big shot. Lots of money. New York. You know.'

'I know,' said Marcus.

'I become a lawyer then I make lots of money and I can help my family. That's what I believe in.'

'God?' said Lydia.

'No,' said the law student, 'I believe in money. That's my god.'

Mustapha looked down at his beer, moved his head from side to side. He wasn't so sure. God still had a place.

'Our mother is very Muslim. You must meet her. She is very Muslim. Very religious.'

Marcus ordered mint tea and the waiter spilled it over him. Hot mint tea.

'Ouch,' said Marcus.

The waiter gestured apologies.

'It's all right,' said Marcus. 'I'll just change my jeans.'

He dripped off to the hotel lobby and up the stairs to their room. He took off his jeans and his thighs were mildly pink from the hot tea. He rolled a smoke quickly and smoked it slowly, looking through the window at the palm trees along the boulevard, hearing the talking and laughter from the restaurant below. As long as everyone was happy he needn't exactly rush back, he could enjoy a smoke, maybe roll a second one and smoke that while he dried out. The flags hung from the lamp standards along the boulevard, a different colour in the street lighting than in daylight. You could make a mistake describing the flag if you only saw it at night.

He went back down. The waiter smiled.

'We have hot showers here.'

'We thought you must be drying yourself,' said the law student. 'Drying your throat.'

Marcus smiled happily. Within the protective cocoon of the m'hashished all was calm. His gums were feeling a bit tender and his lips a bit burnt. He'd looked at the little waterpipes in shop windows but he found it easier rolling joints. Even just rolling them became a pleasurable sensation, delaying the next consumption. And he liked the packets of rolling papers, different sizes, different textures from what he'd been used to. Some people wanted to be big shots, others became connoisseurs of rolling papers.

Mustapha came for them in the morning and they walked up through the colonial town.

'He's a good man,' someone called out as they went past; yesterday's hustler in black smiling at them.

But when they came into the main street a little boy of ten or twelve walked alongside them, 'Don't trust him, he gets a commission from all the shops.'

Mustapha gave the same short chuckle as he gave to the words of recommendation. The little boy bounced up and down and started a running argument with Mustapha, but in the end he dropped back as they carried on along the pavement. They stopped to get tea at one of the pavement cafés, buying cake at the patisserie beside it. Already stoned, and the hunger for sweet things doing its urging. At the next table a group of ageing gays talked and surveyed the scene. They all looked like Christopher Isherwood or William Burroughs. Mustapha gave his short, barking chuckle.

As soon as they'd eaten, Mustapha hurried them on to a cab rank. They drove out to the suburbs. Blocks of apartments, four, five storeys high, the streets unpaved, rutted sand, climbing up and down the undulations of the land, children and youths playing, hanging around, watching them. The room had couches all round it, some blankets folded in one corner, and a large brass tray, table sized. Mustapha put on a record. Jimi Hendrix, winding in through the archway from the next room. His brother had answered the door—'the lawyer', said Mustapha with his short laugh—and then disappeared, either studying or in pursuit of the majouna, verb tense uncertain, explanations ambiguously merging, what had been being done with what was going to be done.

'I had some mushrooms last night,' Mustapha said. 'I bought them from some German students.'

'Good?'

'Good, yes,' he said.

They'd talked about drugs the previous day, how hashish made him too paranoid, how he'd had some acid from Italy. Lydia had recommended mushrooms, gentler than acid.

'Where's your mother?' Lydia asked.

'She's in the kitchen. Cooking.'

'Does she need any help?'

Again the short, barking laugh. 'No, she's all right, she likes to cook.'

'Are you sure?'

'Of course.'

Then the lawyer came through with food, chips, egg,

minced steak. They had expected couscous, tajine. Was this served for them because they were foreigners, tourists, the food they were expected to expect; or was this what they normally ate? Marcus and Mustapha talked about drugs, music.

'Funny,' said Mustapha, 'you are the only person who ever mentions J.J. Cale.'

He put on J.J. Cale. It wasn't just sales talk, the pretence of shared tastes. So across the world you could find people with shared tastes: hashish, Hendrix, J.J. Cale, mushrooms. It added to his relaxation.

The mother didn't join them.

'No, she'll eat later.'

'You mean she cooked this specially for us?' said Lydia.

Mustapha chuckled. 'Of course.'

'So she's been slaving away.'

'Not slaving,' said Mustapha. 'She likes to cook for people.'

Lydia doubted it.

The lawyer produced the majouna, a block about the size of a tin of pipe tobacco. 'We found someone who knows how to make it,' he said. 'Since we are not sure, we found someone who knows.'

'You smoked kif too?' asked Mustapha.

'No, I'd like to.'

'You want some? Forty-five dirhams a bush.'

'What's a bush?'

'That's how they sell it.'

And off went the law student again. He came back with a pipe so they could smoke some there. And then that lighter, speedier stone. The world lit up brighter from the soft, burnished golden somnolence of hashish.

'You tried opium?'

'I tried it once,' said Marcus. 'I rather liked it.'

'Don't get opium here,' said Mustapha. 'If anyone tries to

sell you opium tell them you know what they have here. Hashish and kif. Here there's no opium.'

He went out of the room and came back with a screwed up piece of paper. He opened it out and showed them some shiny, hard black substance.

'Know what it is?'

'No,' said Marcus, sniffing it, feeling it.

'That's what they sell you as opium.'

'But it isn't,' said Lydia.

'No,' he laughed.

'What is it?'

He screwed up his face, what was it? 'They burn it for the smell.'

'Incense.'

'Yes, incense.' He chuckled and rolled it back into its paper and stuffed it into his pocket. He wore tight black jeans, tight t-shirt, but somehow he managed to stash things away into pockets and socks without any revealing indication that he was carrying anything.

'Does your mother mind you smoking?' Lydia asked.

'No, she doesn't mind.'

'Does she know you smoke?'

'Yes, no problem.'

'What about drinking?'

'No, she doesn't know we drink. She wouldn't like that.'

'Does your father smoke?'

'No, not any more. He made the pilgrimage to Mecca, you know, and then you give up things and you don't go back to what you give up.'

Lydia wanted to eat the majouna then, but Marcus wouldn't.

'Let's go back to the hotel and find out how trippy it is. I don't want to be blundering around out of my head somewhere I don't know where I am.'

'It takes an hour to work,' said Lydia.

'Maybe. Maybe not. I'd rather wait till we get back.'

He could see it coming on in the Medina and utter craziness and paranoia taking hold, he didn't want to perceive what the people in the Medina thought about Western tourists, imperialists, infidels, he felt he probably knew, probably agreed with them, he could see himself fractured into warring parts in the bright sun.

They shook hands, they said goodbye to the mother, she came out from the kitchen and they said goodbye, they drifted off along the undulating sandy road, the blocks of apartments standing out with the clear, rectangular, flat look, walls of pastel pinks and greens and whites, and then Mustapha put them into a cab and told the driver where to take them, now they were organised for a while, now they had taken in provisions and needn't venture out again, no more arrangements, no more anxieties, no more doubts.

They ate the majouna which was sweet like a spiced fudge.

'If you want to get higher,' the law student had said, 'you just eat more.'

'To make it work better,' Mustapha had said, 'drink some hot tea.'

So they drank mint tea and walked across the road from the hotel to the beach.

'Chocolat, hachisch?'

'No thank you,' they said.

They walked across the sand to the sea, watching the sand shimmering, the sea resonating. A string of three camels loped across to them.

'You want to ride? You have a ride?'

But they declined. It seemed very high up on the camel's hump, a height out of the dimensions of the heights they were on, no more material, no more precarious, but they felt better with their feet on the ground, indeed Marcus felt better lying perfectly flat on the ground, certainly he had no wish to move or to climb onto something moving. The world's moving was movement enough. He smoked a couple of joints he'd rolled in the hotel. Lydia's eyes glistened, she walked down to the sea to walk in the ripples of the waves. Pale, white English tourists stretched out on towels determinedly getting the sun despite the wind that blew across the sand's surface. 'They are like eggs, the English,' Mustapha had remarked. Marcus watched them frying on the beach.

They walked arm in arm along the sand, Lydia and Marcus, they walked round in a circle, they couldn't find the spot to be, out of the afternoon wind, and the long vistas of stretching beach were luring but long, as they began to walk along it they realised how long it would take to get to the end, so they veered back, describing this erratic circle. They went back to the hotel, leaving the sand to the boys playing football and the frying eggs, chewed some more majouna in the hotel room and looked out at the palm trees, the passers-by in their djellabas, Berber women in their layers of clothing, towelling, and the hustlers walking up and down the street. The palm trees framed by the window were the imprinted image. To see the passers-by you had to stand at the window. But the palm trees were in sight both when you stood at the window and when you lay back on the bed.

They spent a lot of time lying on the bed because they got the usual stomach bug. But though their bowels turned to water, they survived on mint tea and kif and hashish. In a way it suited Marcus, he was quite happy lying down stoned all day, if he had been well he would have felt obliged to go out, wander around, explore, consume, consume. He had enough to consume.

He sat shakily on the hotel's terrace beside the boulevard when he felt strong enough to venture out again, sipping mint tea, picking at a croissant. A boy in black went by and waved. He smiled back cautiously.

'Mustapha's friend,' the boy said, and Marcus remembered bumping into the two of them one day on the street.

Five minutes later Mustapha was there. 'Good morning, how are you?'

'We've been sick, but we're going south tomorrow.'

'You going south, you need some more hash? It's better to buy it here, down there it's more expensive, down there it's harder to get, not like here.'

'Really?'

'Oh yes. Don't trust anybody down south.'

So they went out to the café again, Mustapha's brisk walk, the cab ride, and then the wait. 'Don't trust anybody down south,' Mustapha warned again.

Marcus chuckled, interpreting it as local pride, sales talk maybe.

'No, seriously,' said Mustapha. 'If anybody asks, you don't smoke. Don't give any information.'

Then he went off leaving Marcus at the table in the bare room.

The man came through from the counter.

'Your first time here? You like it? What hotel you stay at?'

Marcus mumbled, Mustapha's warning hanging there, something about the south, going there, arriving from there, as if he was between hotels or something, something anyway so that there was no answer.

The man went back into the other room, came back with an ashtray.

'You smoke?'

'No,' said Marcus.

The man looked at him strangely. 'I leave it,' he said, leaving the ashtray anyway, as if there was some language problem and Marcus wasn't understanding.

Marcus sipped at a soft drink and listened to the music till Mustapha returned.

They took the train south. They struggled along the corridors with their bags and every compartment was occupied; or if there were spare seats the other occupants denied that they were vacant. When they'd reached the end of the train and there were still no seats they sat on the folding seats in the corridor. Five hours on a folding seat in the corridor. But it wasn't as bad as that. When they were clear of the station someone stuck his head out of a compartment and said there were two seats there perhaps. Perhaps if the people who had been there before came back they would have to surrender them; but perhaps the people had now left the train. And so they sat in the compartment, anxious it might only be a temporary seating, but no-one came back and the anxiety seeped away.

He was a student, the one who had offered them seats. He had been studying abroad.

'How did you like it?' Lydia asked.

'The courses are good,' he said. 'But my professor, I think he is a racist. It makes it very difficult. And for my essay on colonialism, he gives me a C because I take a Marxist position.'

'Uh-huh,' said Marcus. No surprises here.

'I think,' said the student, 'there is a kind of double imperialism. First, all our raw materials and products are taken. And second, we have to buy these expensive imports. So we pay both times, both ways we are exploited. I think the people in the rich countries must now share some of their wealth.'

Marcus tried to explain that the people in the rich countries were also exploited, that there was an internal imperialism, the colonised classes were exploited like the colonised nations. Not all the people in the rich countries were rich.

The student shook his head doubtfully. 'But the rich countries, they still have all this wealth which they use to maintain the system here. They pour in aid and it all goes to keep a government that the people do not want in power.'

But Marcus held back, it was not a conversation he wanted; he would have liked it, yes, but knew enough, feared enough, not to pursue it.

'Do you believe in God?' the student asked.

'Yes,' said Lydia.

'And you?'

Marcus nodded.

'And you?' Lydia asked.

'I think,' he said, 'we all come from one source, all the people on the earth.'

'From God,' said Lydia.

The student nodded.

The man in the corner, about fifty, who had pointed out natural salt panning as the train went past, pottery kilns, all the things they passed, which the student translated for them, said something.

'Does he believe in God?' Lydia asked.

The student spoke to him and the man grinned and touched his forehead, the brow over the third eye.

'He says you can see the hollow where he prays, where his head touches the ground.'

The man rolled his trouser legs up to the knees.

'The skin is hardened where he kneels to pray.'

He said something else and the student translated.

'He does not speak English but his son and daughter do. But he speaks Esperanto. He is in communication with forty-five countries. He has Esperanto correspondents in all these countries. He attends the Esperanto conferences in these countries as a delegate.'

The vision of world unity through communication, there on that crowded train: the man with calluses on his knees from praying who spoke the international language that no-one else shared; the woman and child who said nothing; the student—'The only philosophers I think who say anything are Hegel and Marx. The rest, I don't think they say anything to me'; Lydia—'We all come from one source, we are all children of God'; and Marcus, locked in the inexpressible, the things that mattered not to be talked about; and another silent young man who smiled and shared cigarettes but kept out of the conversation; so much silence. But the Esperanto speaker was also a poet. He was committed to reviving and maintaining the traditional folk poetry. The student of Marx translated for them tentatively, was there half a smile on his lips, and yet a respect for the project. 'I had wondered, when I was translating, some of the things he said are hard to translate. I had wondered, yes. But now he explains, he weaves into his conversation this traditional poetry.' Which could not be translated, which remained for Marcus and Lydia with the silent ones. Yet the vision of it, that old and now fading vision of international community, faintly comic as all good and true things now seemed faintly comic, vegetarianism, prayer, pacifism, so that Esperanto was in that category of mild craziness, but outside their own familiar crazinesses and now they had to reconceive their position; for it hung there along with the project for the revival of traditional folk poetry, a vision that Marcus could share but also a fading one for him, how long since he had called up that vision and sat before it, how long since he had surrendered any much hold on that possibility and had accepted unawares the elite specialisation of the marginal man of letters. He could not hear the revived folk poetry. But it was enough, for this moment, to know that it was there, that it was part of this holy man's commitment, that these things could still be believed in and practised with love. 'The

41

true criticism is to create something better,' the student translated, 'the other criticism is—' The gesture of the hand flipped away from the body, and a dismissive sound, a word that Marcus did not catch describing the literary studies he practised, well we all have to practise something, even if we fail to catch the dismissive word for it. 'There is also a cultural imperialism,' he could have begun, 'both internal and colonial.' But he sat silent, listening, this way he heard things and did not talk himself into trouble saying things other people heard. He accepted the holy man's verdict, offered no defence. Who knew what the silent young man was thinking or hearing, who knew what anyone was, always there was this possibility not to be repressed of the inauthentic; even the highest moments in the cocoon of ecstasy had that possibility, that nothing was free from the possibility of this permeation. 'And imperialism is maintained internally and externally by the mechanisms of the police state, of provocateurs and informers, this is what the money poured in as aid goes to maintain.' But it was enough just to think that, not to say it. To maintain it there as a memento. Et in Arcadia ego.

Then further south by road, long bus journeys through stretching brown fields, buildings of earth and stone rising out of the bare brown land, hedges of prickly pear the only vegetation, the land being ploughed with donkeys and camels. And at the bus stops meat grilling at roadside stalls, boys selling bread and hardboiled eggs. Plains, hills, high snow-capped mountains inland, police at the intersections outside the major cities.

Marcus sat drinking mint tea outside a café. It was a tourist resort, there purely for tourists, the old town the other side of the port, quite separate. Huge expensive hotels, big bank buildings, hotels still being built, and older cheap hotels, too.

'How many camels for your wife?'

Two boys at the next table smiling at them. The usual hustle. But they didn't seem to be trying to hustle anything. Down there no-one had come up hustling dope. Marcus was glad he had taken Mustapha's advice and bought another deal. This was a sanitised, hygienised, tourist resort, tourists walking up and down the pavements looking displaced, sleepwalking. Marcus sat there stoned, watching them.

'G.I.s' one of the boys said as three tall, shapeless, gangly figures went by. 'American ship.'

'Here?' Marcus said.

'Yes, came in last night.'

He pulled a face. Just a face. The fatal involuntary reflex.

'English people don't like Americans,' the boy said.

'Not much,' Marcus said. He was about to say, 'who does?' But didn't. 'Don't trust anybody down south,' Mustapha had said.

And now he was down south about to launch into a discussion of American ships.

'See you,' he said to the boys, and paid the bill, and left.

He walked with Lydia through the dusty, sandy park.

'What I hate worst of everything,' he said, 'is having to do that, having to cut off as soon as any conversation might get political.'

'You're getting better at it,' Lydia said.

They had been practising for a while now. They had come to this country as a relief from their practising. But it was no less difficult here.

'So the only conversations you can have are the empty, boring ones. And anyone who looks like they might be interesting, you can't afford to talk to. Anyone who looks like they might agree with you, you have to suspect at once of being a provocateur. It makes it very hard to go on.'

Off the beach the submarine was moored, the black outline breaking the water's surface, Leviathan rising. The aircraft skimmed in over the sand to the tourist airport, the runways ready for any military contingency. Inland the guerillas encroached on the desert boundaries. At the airport when they flew back all the baggage was deposited on the runway beside the aircraft. Passengers had to identify their own bags before they were loaded on board. It was all around them, the inexorable process. Marcus smoked as much hashish as he could absorb before they left; the days of the imperialist decadence were surely numbered, who knew how long it would be so freely available?

Singing Birds

These were the great days for poets. The heroic days. The days of myth. When the clock was always at quarter to three in the morning. They rolled on the pavements like alchemical twins, breaking each others' heads into the awaiting concrete. They howled their way through plate glass doors and windows. Their blood congealed. Their cars caught fire. When their clothes were taken they wore their neckties. Naked meant honest, as in lunch, dead, cop. For emperor's new clothes they wore sombreros and smoking jackets. They brandished machine guns and straddled mustangs. They shot themselves and others, possessed explosives, attempted assassination, did smash and grabs, died from dirty needles. Waste not, want not, drug poems, prison poems, to say nothing of the madhouse. Nothing will be said of the madhouse.

He was a policeman with the soul of a poet. Or a poet with the soul of a policeman. And who is to say which had priority? A literary agent who could book you. Some people grew moustaches, long hair, shark's tooth medallions, sunglasses, key rings at the hip, the janitorial touch, the payroll guards. 'This is your cover,' they said, giving him a jacket with his picture on the back. 'Start a magazine,' they said, 'get funding from the bored. Make it glossy, sticky, tacky, everyone will want to get into your pages, we'll supply the boys and girls.' They always supplied the boys and girls. 'Then you print the poems and the boys or girls say how they dig the poems and then they get to screw the poets. That's the only way we can be sure to get the poets screwed. Mediated through art.'

He would have preferred it if they'd paid for sex but this was bohemia and he was told that love like verse had to be free. 'But you can deal a little dope,' they said, 'they'll pay for that, get them hooked, that would be a service. Like the massage parlour girls, get them hooked, make them pay back their earnings for dope. You supply the dope so they can write the sort of stoned shit you publish in the magazine,' they said. 'And you get to introduce the chicks,' they said, 'you'll be the M.C. as it were. Macho Chap. You heard of the big banana and the big potato and the big pineapple, well you're the big stud and you don't even have to wear a collar.'

There were poets declaiming Rimbaud in the café noirs, revolution was plotted in their cups and recorded in the potted palms. Coups were conceived over the cheesecake and captured in the kitchen. There were poets' balls, barbecues of skewered kidneys, acid in the punch, sexual harassment institutionalised and licensed. There were anthologies of desire and manifestoes of will. Proclamations of ego and performances of id. Speaking in tongues, computerised address lists, minimum fees, cash enslavement, questionnaires on the lone and level sands. State your poetics, state your politics. The poetry of pure sound.

The logic required whole huts of poets writing out material for him. For when he became famous. Success might catch him up. A book. Another book, they demand another book, follow it up. He put his mind to the organisational problems. Translations from the Italian. Get the semioticians to program the poetry machine. Telepathic theft. All he had to do was get some telepathine and that wasn't difficult.

'Nothing's too difficult for us,' they told him. They had their men out there combing the hairs of the jungle for telepathine.

'Invite the writers round,' they said, 'feed them chemicals allowing easy transfer of information and plunder their word hoard.' The first experiment made him sick. The psyches.

'So how do I write it?' he said. 'There has to be a better way.'

'We'll send you the lines,' they said, 'install a telex, we've got a line service, we send lines all round the world, we'll fax you.'

'But then they'll know they're not mine.'

'No they won't, they never read, poets never read other people's poetry and the public doesn't read it at all. Anyway, we only send any given set of lines to one person per major language group, more or less.'

'What if they get translated?' he said.

'They'll sound different. That's the point about poetry, it's not what you say but the way you say it, as they say.'

'But what about what you say, though?'

'Well, you don't say very much, it's all a matter of style. The less you say the better, really.'

'Ah,' he said.

'That's right,' they said, 'a sound poem.'

He tried it again, 'Ah.'

'Well done,' they said. 'Least said, soonest mended. Never overdo the content, that's how you tell a subversive, by the content.'

'What sort of content?' he said.

'Any sort of content,' they said. 'Just content's subversive in itself.'

'Protection,' he said.

'Protection,' they said.

'So if I deal the dope?'

'Protection,' they said. 'As long as we supply it.'

'Of course,' he said. 'I wouldn't dream of dealing with anyone else.'

THIS IS FOR YOU

'Don't do it either,' they said.

'What about poems?'

'What about poems?'

'Protection for bad poems.'

'That's your look out,' they said. 'We'll fix the reviews but in the day-to-day fisticuffs of the poets' café, you're on your own. But if they kill you for your bad verses, we'll revenge you,' they said. 'Never fear, if they get you, we'll get them, don't worry about it.'

'Thanks,' he said.

'You're welcome,' they said. 'Don't mention it. We'd be glad of a chance to off a few poets if you disappear. Writing about civil rights and human rights and land rights and race riots and wars and rumours of war and conspiracies. Some of them need to be done over every once in a while, hey man, have some of this superdope, what a blast, sprayed with skunk oil, guaranteed to drive everyone away from you for six months; no man, we can't have that old skunk-oil smoker on the program, he's just too much.'

But this was all low level stuff. His poet's soul wanted more job satisfaction. He studied the aesthetics of it. Get the right recipe and funding will flow. He rebelled against traditional forms. He developed an insignia of the modern. It seemed radical but looked at in the right light it was all right. 'Just challenge the old, the established, the traditional literary order. We've got our chaps there, we need you with the enemy. What the old money won't publish through their traditional firms and established quarterlies is yours.' And when he was on his own, or better still when he had people round, so they could see him actually doing it, he would chisel out a poem or two. Or the odd line thereof. Written on the plaster of a broken arm or a broken wall. Or the frame of a painting, the ripped out title page of a book, a piece of bone or vellum. 'Would you like us to print up some menus?' they said, 'so you can create on them,' these men in button down shirts, watching their work being done.

So there was always dope around at his place, always chicks, sometimes they'd have a barbecue and roast a dead sheep or a side of an ox. Connections with the meat trade. But the troubadors always embellished the story. 'We drove out to the plains and caught one and hit it over the head till it died and put it in the boot of the car.' Just like getting chicks. Machismo like they promised, poet's licence to kill, rape and shoplift with impunity.

It wasn't too bad being a poet. A different beat but the same old drummer. It didn't take too much time. Not many words. And no-one cared anyway. No-one needed to understand it. So it wasn't too bad. When you got into it you realised the possibilities of faction. Sexual play. With this poet's lady, and let him know. But a slip of the tongue. The oral tradition. Who's been sleeping in whose bed. 'I thought you guys had a liberated scene.' Get them stoned, get them pissed, bring them home and listen to the bastards. 'Here, smoke some of this supergrass and give us the full story.' A change from watching TV. Here you could write your own plots. Anyway, you could always watch TV at the same time, secure in the knowledge that everything was being taped anyway, he didn't even have to stay awake.

The Imagination

W hen someone rings the door-bell and then hammers the knocker and then beats against the timber itself, or glass or whatever, in this case it was a timber door, and an old iron knocker, and a clockwork bell, all three going together, more or less, if you're feeling extroverted and wanting excitement maybe you leap up and answer it to whoever is announcing 'Where's the party?' 'Come in, my dear, you are the party.' Who wouldn't want a leather-clad silver-studded rapist with a knife climbing in, what an exquisite and so international a literary fantasy. But the leather and stud boys all go across the road and down the steps to the house on the water's edge, Mr Bonmot's, dressed to kill for the weekend, cruising butchers and doctors on their Harley Davidsons.

So the threefold knocking at the door is not unfamiliar, it has something of that overdetermination characteristic of certain literary schools and lifestyles. At least the door is closed. I might have left it open and had them just walk in. Sam clutching his bottle of tia maria or ave atquavita, southern comfort or northern desperation, not at all a great western champagne type, with in his other hand maybe a fish or two, hanging there from a hook like souls being weighed on judgement day, their tails occasionally twitching in some involuntary electric retching orgasm, and in another hand some chick person clutched by the hobbled anklets or neck feathers, some nubile gesture of asserted heterosexuality though getting on the weird side, approaching the underage size, or maybe it was just the short dresses like school tunics, one of those zombie non-persons he brings round like they've eaten blowfish and are now under his command, buried alive and born again, 'Sam, Sam, I am your willing slave, my eyes are dead but my life goes on and as for the imagination, the imagination Sam, imagine the imagination,' Sam, Sam, surrender a hand and find us a verb, what are you doing, Sam, out on the doormat where Marcus the mouser deposits disembowelled mouse carcases?

And it swells there, the great inflation of the imagination, the undirectable dirigible, 'Let's go and knock on somebody's door, ring their doorbell, hammer their windows, wood, iron and glass, when shall we three meet again, the imagination is Sam's broomstick, his horse's head handle to prod the lions of deconstruction, his musket to pick up and straddle. 'What I like about you is when I come round in the middle of the night and you're pissed off you don't pretend you're not. I go round and see The Egg at three in the morning and he offers me coffee and omelettes, imagine it. Imagine it. And I know he's pissed off. That's why I go round there and get him out of bed.' The Egg fingers his moustache and rises tip toe on his built-up heels. Are they angled right for the ascent of Olympus? Will icicles form on the words that will issue from his lips? Sam is impervious. He takes the icicles to pack the fish. He drinks from the built-up heels. He would crack alabaster boxes over them if asked, and maybe has. Literature's shoeshine boy. He smiles up at me. Through the window beside the door.

MOVIE ADDICTION

I don't want to see Sam. And fish. And chick person. I want to watch this trio of horror movies scripted by the man who scripted *Psycho*. I've never seen *Psycho*. I don't like horror movies. I have combed through the television guide and *Movies on TV* to find something there might be a remote reason for watching. Movies consisting of three-separate stories, three vaguely related subplots or unrelated variations on a theme, etc., are rarely satisfying. I find. This is all from my perspective. I found. At that point in time. My perspective then. Though my views on those three-sectioned movies haven't changed. Other things have. Changed. Tonight, now, I am not watching a remake of *Invasion of the Body Snatchers* nor a remake of *The Big Sleep*. Though once I might have. The originals, then it might have been different; but it is not the originals and instead I am recalling this incident of the evening I was watching the Robert Bloch trilogy. Thanks for the counterfeit, the ersatz, the substitutes, the remakes: then we don't have to bother with them. As more of our world becomes ersatz, remade, substitute, food, entertainment, politics, fiction, the less we bother with it. This has some truly revolutionary implications. The negation of the negations.

'No, Sam,' I say, 'I'm watching a movie, no.'

'Why're you watching a movie when you could be talking with a real flesh and blood human being?'

Blood has already been inserted into the picture.

'For the reason Americans eat brand name fast foods,' I answer him. 'It may not be real food but you know what to expect. Hamburgers and movies for those who want to live safely.'

'There's a human being out here.'

'Where?'

'I just want to talk to you. Like old friends. Remember about friends. What people used to have. I thought we could be friends. I thought we were friends. We are friends. Aren't we?'

FRIENDSHIP

Is this what E.M. Forster was thinking of when he said he hoped he'd have the courage to betray his country rather than his friend? Sam out there, howling protestations of friendship, a greater writer than any of them and probably no worse a friend than Bloomsbury or Kings Coll. Cantab. could offer. Friendship, I decide, is a peculiarly bourgeois concept. In the world of work there are mates, comrades, fellows; lovers, partners, in the world of sex. Who are these friends with whom you neither work nor make love? Wasn't Marcus Brutus Caesar's friend? An appeal to friendship is not an open sesame round here.

But doesn't Sam know that? Doesn't he know that will keep him on the windswept porch, a beautiful view of the harbour, maybe he could even see the television through the window, but cold out there, as I remember it was cold out there. So he can have the exquisite joys of exclusion, denial, friendship revealed as hollow when it comes to letting him in. Now at his most excluded he most exists and is most present. He rises up at the window like some overbearing djinn. 'Go back inside your bottle,' I order him. But he's probably swallowed the cork. Now we are stuck with him like a dispersed noxious vapour that has penetrated everything. Asmodeus and the fishy fume. It's not that he's doing a lot of hammering on doors after his first arrival. Nor even being especially vocal. But sitting there. Like Quasimodo without a bell rope. And you know or fear that at any moment he will call out or strike, how can you relax to a horror movie of hands being severed by meat cleavers as they come through walls or electric cables being attached to metal door handles ready for visitors, how can you relax and flow into this with Sam at the door?

'What should I do then?' he asks. 'Should I phone first?'

'You could try.'

'But you never answer it, there's never anyone there when I ring.'

'I must be psychic.'

'That's cruel,' says Sam. 'Why are you so cruel? What have I ever done to you?'

We are not going to begin that enumeration. You can't catch old birds with chaff. We are not going to get sucked into an itemised account of all the things Sam has done to me or not, with arguments, variants, extenuating circumstances and maybe even witnesses.

'I brought these for you,' he says, holding the fish to the window.

'I don't eat fish, I'm a vegetarian.'

'No you're not.'

'I'm a Midlander. We never saw fish.'

'You never saw lots of things,' said Sam. 'Here's your chance to see fish.'

He presses a fishy eye against the window. Maybe he didn't have fish. Maybe that was another time. Maybe he was just drunk. Maybe he just rang the doorbell and hammered the knocker and banged the door too loud.

'Just open the window,' says Sam.

'Why?'

'I want to talk to you. I can't talk with the door shut. I won't try to come in, promise.'

Would I have thought he would try to come in if he hadn't said he wouldn't? Yes, I would, that is why it is the window that is at issue, not the door. He doesn't even try about the door. The door will not be opened.

I open the window. Is this remorse at such unfriendliness? Is this weakening, what Sam sees as weakening? I have calculated I can easily push him out before he climbs through, and if he is appropriately positioned a push might send him rolling down the stairs. Even somersaulting. It is

these violent fantasies that betray me. I have not calculated
that he will simply put his arm through the open window
and leave it there, hanging.

'Move it, Sam.'

He leaves it there.

'Why do you want your arm there?'

'It's not hurting anything,' says Sam, 'I'm not breaking in.'

'Then take your arm out.'

These lines are inevitably perfunctory, since he doesn't, and
we both know he won't take the arm out.

'Sam,' I say at some point, 'if you don't go I'll call the
cops.'

What a bad idea in every regard, it is hardly worth
suggesting.

'That would be great,' says Sam, Sam the Overjoyed,
'they've still got a couple of warrants they've never cancelled
out for me, you call the cops and I get taken off to Long Bay
and then it's an automatic three years for a habitual offender,
that would look great, wouldn't it, the man who puts Sam
Samson back in jail, that would look great in the literary
histories, wouldn't it?'

It's the bit about the literary histories that makes me feel
this is getting out of control. Maybe I should just open the
door suddenly and roll him down the stone and concrete
steps, about fifteen of them, better heads, or at least other
heads, than his have bled on those stone steps, the time when
Ms Kiss-me Kate crashed down them and split her head
open a bit and demanded we took her, they took her, to her
psychiatrist. 'Are you sure this is the right sort of head
doctor?' Tony Leanto her publisher asking anxiously all the
way. But Sam of course might split open too far and who
would want to be on a manslaughter charge for Sam, just to
watch a horror movie?

Kitchen knives are sawing through wrists, fabric and

rubber insulated wires are stripped back to the gleaming metal ready for insertions too distasteful to look at. I turn back to Sam. Why does he provoke this violence in me, Sam who never strikes a first blow? The master of provocation. Do you like being punched, Sam, is that your Swinburnian secret, so there is no way of winning with you except by beating you into unconsciousness which for you is what you want, I fall upon the thorns of life, I bleed, you are not someone who only fights to win and otherwise keeps away, you are as happy to fight to lose, for loss means the exquisite pummelling. Or is this just a psychological profile cunningly circulated so people don't punch you because it seems so obviously not worth while. Who can tell the forger from the coin? Sam gives his angelic smile.

The arm still hangs there.

'I'll shut the window on it.'

'That's why it's there,' says Sam, 'so you won't shut the window. I want to talk.'

'Talk then, just take your arm out.'

He neither talks nor takes his arm out.

It is a sash window. I bring it down on his arm. His arm stays there. I raise the window and bring it down again, harder this time. By the third time I have got the hang of it, got into the swing of things, I've got rhythm. But though the movement is like a guillotine the edge is blunt. The arm remains there, no wrist lopped off into the room. There are worse things going on on the television screen, but they are only acted. As far as we know. Maybe much of this is only acted. But I happen to be one of the actors and it is not nice stuff. Not nice to recall, either. Not much to look forward to in re-run. Sam, we are so aware of your chameleon qualities and your mimetic skills that we assume your manipulations are of flattery for your own ends; but sometimes it seems you let us hold the mirror to our own worse selves, and is this therapeutic, cathartic, is this for us to reform from?

In the end I disgust myself as he knows I will.

I phone La Surreal. 'Come and get your rotten husband,' I say, maybe something other than rotten, but after fighting for those freedoms of expression all these years and probably generally losing or only marginally gaining, set back from what we might have gained, anyway, we are back to rotten again.

'I can't,' she says, 'he's got the car.'

'Get a cab,' I say.

'We haven't got any money.'

'Borrow some from a friend.'

'You're our only friend,' she says.

I would like to go aaargh and rip out the phone cord from the wall to a rending, blinding flash, yellow on purple background, wham, bam, slam, etc., like comics, like television. The television has people wired up to naked cables. The window frame has Sam leaning through like a chambermaid above a flower-box of geraniums in *La Bohème*, a limp arm like a red setter's tongue, spam, pretenderised deboned boiled in its own juice ham. Probably whale blubber. The great fat bat of a whale penis.

And in the background the harbour, prawn trawlers, cargo ships laden with timber from Borneo, Samarcand, all the ready visual enhancement and exotic associations. In that ugly brick block across the water someone paints jacarandas in bloom. And the bridge grips the two points of land like a tourniquet on a junky's arm. 'Bullshit,' Sam would say, would have said, and he should know about that.

NEXT MORNING

Next morning the phone rings and it is La Surreal, this early morning cocorico with great red wattles vibrating like they are powered by an electric vibrator, plugged into the mains, all 240 volts aglow.

'You must be proud of yourself,' she says.

'Oh, I dunno,' I say.

'Sam's at the hospital.'

'What, the nuthouse?' I say, not my normal parlance but called for at this point, provided, anyway.

'You've broken his arm.'

'I hope so.'

'It's being x-rayed now.'

'Use the x-ray for the cover of his next book,' I suggest. They are into snazzy design.

'It's his writing arm. He can't use his hand.'

'Then tell him to use feet. Give up free verse and stick to pentameters.'

Bullshit it's his writing arm, he's got another one, he types two-handed on his electric typewriter, a gigantic IBM behind which he shelters like Dr Phibes of Black Mountain, summoning up pterodactyls on the carillon. Though what he really wants is a keyboard and synthesiser, pouring out his full soul in profuse streams of unpremeditated art like Shelley, a four track, an eight track, so he could work over it afterwards, something to do at night and keep him off the streets.

'What's he going to do now?' asks La Surreal.

'The imagination,' I say, 'tell him, the imagination.'

This Is for You

S
he made him a puppet before they split up. An exact replica of him as far as a stuffed rag doll can be an exact replica. An exact caricature. Just reduced, shrunken. However you formulated it, you knew it was him. There was no intention of disguising it. It wasn't pretending to be other than him. She had made it as an image of him. Or in his image, as it were. That was why she had given it to him.

'This is for you,' she said. This is of you. This is you. Almost a case of 'This Is Your Life'. Clasped in her bony fingers there.

So he unwrapped it from its brown paper wrapping, that austere lack of frippery so characteristic of her, and there it was. There he was. Looking up. Like Narcissus in the pond.

It was a matter of recognising it rather than falling in love with it. Recognising himself, he had to guard against this alienation of seeing himself as it. Seeing the puppet as it was was fair enough. A correct perception. Except that since it was a puppet of him, to see it as it was to slip into those alienations. While to say, 'That is me' was another way, too, of seeming to be somewhat schizoid. A divided self. L'autre, c'est moi. He'd be getting a personalised numberplate on his car next. OTHER.

The limp nature of the rag doll aspect of the simulacrum distressed him a bit. He didn't feel that limp. It made him feel limper than he really felt. And it had been made that way, it hadn't just got that way over the years of having had the stuffing knocked out of it. It came limp.

There was no need to see it as in any way sinister. It was simply the fact of their having broken up that suggested a possible acrimony and the suggested acrimony made him wonder if there were any other intent there in the manikin other than the production of a craft object. Like, was it malign? If you stuck pins in it and lit wax candles before it, would he feel the pricks in his own body? And if so where should he place the pins? Where did he want to be pinpricked? It was not a question he could easily put to himself. What was worse, to seem to catch yourself wondering about the reality of witchcraft or to find yourself considering whether your former friend was into it? Nor was this something that could ever be asked, certainly not of her, and who else would be able to answer?

So he stuck it out of the way on top of the bookcase and the particles of dust settled on it over the days and weeks and years, giving the hair a grey tinge, the face a flaky texture.

Anyway it wasn't the fear of pin sticking. Since he had the puppet there the only person in a position to do any pin sticking was him, and he wasn't going to do that, not even for experiment. The cost of finding out some things is too great. Or might be too great. So with it stuck up in the corner there, there was no reason not to feel quite secure. It was just that he would have liked to have got rid of it. Seeing it, him, reminded him of her and he didn't especially want such memories. He would have liked just to have tossed it out. Into the garbage. But he was held back by this fear of some awful consequence. Just the possibility that it might emblematically presage his own downfall. It certainly didn't seem to be something worth risking. Not just to get rid of a rag doll. So it stayed there. Up above the books. He couldn't stuff it away in a cupboard and suffocate it. It had to have reasonable conditions. Able to breathe. Look around. Look down at him. Exchange a glance. Year after year he exchanged glances with it. Which made him think that maybe it did have some force. Not necessarily a malign force. Not necessarily sucking his energy. Not necessarily needing placating. Yet it worried him, registering it, resenting it; if he could not fully accept it then he might as well have stuck pins in it. Or tossed it on the open fire. There was no point in pretending to conceal his resentment. It was as if it knew. At least if he'd tossed it on the fire that would have been a quick solution, instead of this slow hatred, reflected back and forth, the motes illuminated in the rays of sunlight between him and his image, me and my doll, his master's voice, something he dared not destroy, something that was going to be with him till the end, till the end of one of them. Which one was immaterial, the end of one would be the end of the other, whichever went first, the other would follow, tossed on the flames. And only then would they really know which one was to go first.

He thought of giving it back to her. But that would have meant communicating with her. And he didn't want to do that. And she might have taken it amiss. Returning her gift. Then there could well be a disaster. A holocaust. As she stuffed the returned puppet into her pot-bellied stove. It was safer to keep it than to give it back. Or to give it to anyone else. Who knew what tricks they might try with it? Hanging it by its neck as a comic *objet d'art*. Giving it to a puppy as a plaything. It wasn't something that you cared to let out of your possession. Though he wouldn't have minded it out of his sight. He didn't take it on trips with him. It looked down when he was packing but he rejected the plea. He didn't want it suffocating in the suitcase. And going away, it was good to be away from it. A new life. But whenever he visualised his room when he was away, it was there. His representative. The guardian of his territory. The dutiful doppelgänger. The house of clay in residence while his astral body roamed. He always returned to it. His familiar.

61

Red Rock

Those who hold good teachings in respect, see in common trees and stones all the beautiful lights and colours of lapis lazuli, while greedy people, who do not know enough to control their own minds, are blind even to the splendours of a golden palace.

These were the times of promotion. The frenzy of column inches and airplay. We gave interviews. We gave comments on favourite words, New Year's resolutions, how we worked. Anything that came in we did. The constant flurry of traffic along the wires, onto the keyboard. What I said I can't remember. Treading a line between trying to please and trying to tell the truth. The truth as it then appeared. And to tell too much truth meant failing to please. And pleasing meant telling too little truth. But in the flurry there was no time to rest and think about it. And amidst it these promoters were themselves into their own promotion. Gloria came into town with her new program. She had a program in one big city, now she was moving up to do it in a bigger city. To do both. All joined together by landlines. She needed to sell her image as a new program. So there I am, tentatively, nervously wandering into a downtown block to meet her, and there she is in a plastic cubicle with a plastic desk and talking on two phones and gesturing to sit down, and of course sex is all part of it, there is a risqué quality to her product, straight talking about sex, that sort of sexploitation, so the male market all wants to fuck her, who is so challenging and contentious and

independent, strong-voiced, loud, supermanic but controlled, and then I'm offered a coffee while I wait by someone
in tight denim, Gloria is in brown business-person career-
person gear, this other in tight jeans, tight denim shirt with
those top one two three buttons undone so I am looking in
that direction, ordering coffee, and more than that I don't
recall. The green plastic, the brown shirt and brown knitted
jumper, the blue denim.

Here am I just a young writer hustling promotion for a
book so I am not going to be fucking Gloria, it doesn't seem
to me, she's in another league it seems, but the girl who
brings me coffee in a nervous tentative way, I assume she
must be the coffee bringer, her nervousness and tentativeness
are greater than mine so I put her in that category, always we
are putting people in categories because if you don't know
who they are, how do you know whether you should hustle
them or not, those innocent years of talking to everyone,
anyone, gazing into their eyes for the moment of intimate
connexion, but now it is assumed all that has been done in
the writing and now the time is for hustling not connexions
of tenderness, soulbeauty. But still sex, the sweet smell of
success has some sweet musky odour of sexuality incor-
porated into it. And that is what the girl who brings me
coffee in a nervous tentative way also brings. She is
tremulous on the edge of exuding sexuality, does she get to
fuck the ones Gloria turns down, is that it? Or checks them
out like a poison taster. And then Gloria is off the phones
and exuding charm and chaos, utter chaos, everything is
going wrong with the program, the landline went dead this
morning for three minutes just when the general manager
was listening to it driving in to the office, and there are
people who don't like the idea of the program anyway
jumping at any chance to sabotage it, inter-city rivalries,
political factions, leagues of decency ready to leap, and the

coffee bringer sits on the edge of the desk and Gloria introduces her, this is Martha my producer, and the idea of fucking a producer is equally as inhibiting as fucking Gloria for just a young writer, here we are, two books out, maybe three, maybe it's the third I'm hustling, the one people say they don't understand, everything teetering at this moment of precarious balance.

And then they rush off for some promotion or other and I wave goodbye as they flurry off, have to rush, come along to this thing tonight. And I go home for the gentle afternoon, the grey drizzle falling softly on the ships moored in the harbour, black huddled ships, red just above the waterline, but then black above the red, and white bridges, ships from Japan and Greece and Germany and England and America. A soft grey afternoon, bulbuls in pairs on the powerlines, chirruping to each other.

We get drunk at the bar on the free booze and then we go on but where we went I can't recall. Maybe another promotional party. I remember drinking in a bar, sitting with Martha and is it because someone has said something, my own producer, my own promoter, my own agent who is with me there looking for fun too in her own promotional frenzy of predatory enthusiasm, otherwise we'll have to fuck each other, these are the days of huge sexual energy and no time to stop and ask who is it, why is it, so maybe she said Martha was interested or maybe just I should crack on to Martha, this is the age of brusqueness, taut economy, maybe Gloria said something, you've got a fan in Martha, these are the details never remembered or always repressed, these are the times of the good life, booze, sex, promotion, fame, fame the culmination everyone is hurling themselves at, mad, crazed, bug-eyed blinded moths hurtling towards the perpetual flame of fame.

Gloria has a man in tow, a policeman become playwright,

she had a flair, Gloria, for being a step ahead; at a time when prison poets and prison playwrights were in fashion, she found a rarer category; we were all in categories, both us and her. Off they go, and off Martha and I go, the sitting on the bar stools looking into eyes phase, again unremembered, recreatable yet unknown, must have done it, some time or other, no she won't come back to my place, I want to be there in case my girlfriend phones, she is out of town, hustling something for some program as I recall, and may phone. I don't want not to be there. Martha seems to think she might arrive back in person, seems to have misunderstood, wants to go to her hotel, I recoil from hotels, as a young nervous writer I always feel like an interloper, and not only in hotels, but she wins, that's where we go back to.

This is the hotel I vowed never to enter, bounced at the door when I tried to go in for a drink after getting bored with a big anti-war demonstration outside, mass occasions holding no joy and on principle I probably agreed with everything said, why endure hearing it, I do not need to be converted, and this clearly obvious to the doorman, who grabs me by the collar and pushes me back and I try to enter again and it looks like he's going to take a thump at me but some media people save me, intervene, and I'm taken back into the demonstration, this maybe ten years earlier, I vow revenge, and now I'm in there with Martha, afraid yet again of being bounced, what happened to the decision never to enter? Sex triumphs over hate, that is good, everything that triumphs over hate.

And again, amongst the things not remembered, is fucking, not to begin with, or end with, but at one point we stand beside the window there, draw back the blinds, up on the fourteenth or twenty-fourth floor, naked there looking down at the minute figures in the empty square, a fountain, a few people, and we fuck there standing in the window looking down at the square and hopefully looking in each other's eyes too, 'Oh, you're into exhibitionism are you,' she says, just a comment, no opinion one way or another.

And woken by a phone call for me, she takes it, it's a woman for me, she's freaking, it's my own personal promoter, she doesn't mind, it's not that sort of scene I assure Martha.

'She was looking at me last night,' says Martha, hand over phone.

'It's okay,' I say, 'it's probably business, tell her I'm here, it might be important.'

She finally gives me the phone, doubtful.

'She left her briefcase in my car,' I explain. 'She phoned early to make sure of finding me.'

Martha groans in the grey morning. Hangover time.

She gives me a red rock, a translucent piece of quartz. From the West. She was given it when doing a program there.

What is this, a rock?

They go back to the other city. I use the rock as a paperweight. Then I read that minerals and colours draw down planetary influences, and objects can have talismanic powers. I throw out everything that might bring down harmful or unhelpful influences, my little Mexican god, my Niugini Blackwater River head, my Balinese carving of the man with a prick as big as himself, and my rock. Five, six, seven years later. And this morning I started to read Jack Kerouac and like every time I read Kerouac I put down the book, whichever book, and want to write, always his note is the note of memory and search and wanting to write it as close to as it was as you can dare, as at this stage you can try, and outside the rain is a soft grey drizzle over the gentle harbour, and ships from the coast, from Germany, from China moored there, *Mulheim*, *Iron Mittagong*, *Bai He Kou*, and a booklaunch party this afternoon I shall not be going to, these are other days now, calmer days when we can reflect on the flurried days, if anything from the flurry lodged deep enough to be recalled, yet not so deep as to be denied. And it would be nice to think that in that flurried haze there was some moment of true light, some authentic warming glow, some occasion of true contact, pink translucent quartz, momentary, but so is it all, all momentary.

Midnight Readings

Fifteen years later as I was reading poetry in a MacDougal Street coffee-house for free, he was there tape-recording the whole thing and I recognized him immediately but in the gaiety of poetry just put my fist under his chin and said 'You, I remember you, bosun, what are you doing taking all this down?' As I saw his crewcut and tweed jacket I realized now, fifteen years later, 1959, that he was some kind of investigator for the government. He must have remembered my name over the fifteen years and figured I was a Communist, maybe the Navy told him about my interview with Naval Intelligence at Newport R.I. I've always had the feeling the F.B.I. is watching me, or the like, because of my bum record in the Navy, tho I'm still proud of having had the highest I.Q. in the history of Newport Naval Base.

JACK KEROUAC, *VANITY OF DULUOZ*

Yellow light reflecting on the surface of the water, the throbbing dynamo of the tanker right across the harbour, its stern lit up like the grand hotel protruding from behind a point of land covered with gums, and a cicada hurtling through the night air and settling on your leg as you sit on the step, watching the view and the street. And the mosquitoes settling, less welcome than the clinging cicada. You light a couple of joss sticks of incense and move just inside the door and you watch the light shimmer on the water from the naval base opposite across the harbour. Wars and rumours of wars, are these the last days again? Another floating restaurant floats by, festooned with yellow light. You wonder whether to phone the girl you met a few days ago. Five nights ago. You take up the crystal ball that used to hang from the chinese paper lanterns and break up the sunlight into prismatic fragments. You hold it by its cotton thread and ask, yet once more, is she a police agent, and it revolves clockwise, and you wonder if you are manipulating it, if it was a free response. It also says yes when you ask if it's all right to phone her, but when you ask more specifically is it all right to phone her now it swings anti-clockwise. Little prawning boats scuttle up and down the harbour, little trawlers, the cicada sits still, a sailing dinghy with its high mast and no sail cruises upstream under power, just two lights showing on its slim, skeletal frame.

Yesterday you were reading Balzac to understand your life, to find a model to decode your world. You don't remember the phone call precisely. Not the exact words. They asked was it you, they had your name. In future you have to ask who's speaking. After you'd got the message it was too late to ask, it would have sounded too anxious, too paranoid. So the caller asks if it's you and you say yes. State Parliament, he says. Are there two people of that name, your name? And you assume somehow, no reason, just sloppily, filling in the lacunae, that this must be the parliamentary library and they have some cataloguing query, you are reading Balzac, the literary life, but it isn't that, they want to know if you have just died or if that was another writer of the same name. No, there isn't another writer of the same name as far as you know, there was an actor, he died about eighteen months ago or was it two years or five years ago, time foreshortens down here on the coast, did he die of a heroin overdose? A heart attack or something, you say. 'No, this writer,' the caller says, 'this writer of your name died of a heroin overdose about five days ago.' 'Never touch the stuff,' you say, 'no, I'm still alive.' This is where you ask who did you say was phoning. 'State Parliament,' he says, what you'd thought he'd said. 'Yes, we've got a lot of time on our hands, I've got a couple of officers down here having a bet on it, one of them's going to be very mad, there's a lot of money on it, well thank you for your time.'

'Maybe they were reading next week's press release,' says your colleague who does work for the police department when you go to afternoon tea.

'If anything happens to me, remember,' I say.

'I wish you hadn't told me,' he says.

I could phone the switchboard and see if they know anything about the call but I don't see much future in that. I don't see that much future anywhere.

So if I am being warned, what am I being warned about? Is this a threat? Or is it just a story going round, another story going round, everyone so freaked by heroin it leaves a taint? And this man with two officers phoning me up.

The last person who offered me heroin we figured was a police agent. And here he is on the phone, two days after the night with the girl, asking for a cutting from my newspaper files, the first I've heard from him for six months, since I figured he was a police agent and decided to distance myself. I mail him the cutting, or photocopy thereof, so we don't have to encounter each other's eyes.

This is crazy stuff. This is why I'm reading Balzac. Balzac who puts Vautrin central to his *Comédie Humaine*. Vautrin aka Vidocq, the ex-informer, the ex-crim, who becomes head of security, Vautrin the node, the focus, the ever-watching eye, the man of power, and isn't it still like that but everyone forgot to tell me?

Maybe it is not the girl, or maybe it is, that brings this

thick cloud of darkness down, the context in which I met her has its own blackness anyway, all these things happening and a few more. Off in the endless pursuit of dope, the heads in which you can see the crystals of THC shining, man, 'Look at them,' says Luke my early morning visitor, waking me up at first light it seems, that was two weeks ago that sample and the deal still hasn't shown, the great dope deal in the sky. We go to meet the man, it still hasn't shown, we go to meet the man, looks the part of a dealer, hat and earring and all, a little bit of the sixties surviving, we sit at the bar being cool, oblique, it hasn't come through. 'Been working on your car?' says the man. 'What?' says Luke. The man gestures at some black on Luke's wrist. 'No, painting,' says Luke, though you could see how it could look like grease if you were looking for clues, practising reading the signs. The signs of people who are noticeably observant, these are the worrying signs. And then someone comes up to you at the bar and says someone at work said you'd had a heart attack but it turned out to be someone else, the same name again, dying like flies. The person who tells you laughs. Uproariously is how it's always put. You both laugh uproariously, though you less so. That was the night before you met the girl.

The cicada must have exhausted itself in its freak out. It hasn't moved from its sticky grasp on my leg since it settled, not croaked or squeaked or fidgeted, just clung on there. The incense seems to discourage the mosquitoes. My head is aching a bit, which could be auric contamination; writing about all this draws in the blackness. Maybe put the note pad down and prune a few more leaves off the secret dope plants to clear the head, give a little buzz, before writing about the girl.

I watched Dustin Hoffman's first role in a movie, just a spot on the midday movie on TV. All the sixties movies that bombed, that were panned, ditched, dumped, sabotaged, now appear on midday television, bought in packages with the expensive stuff that gets the ratings, and this weird stuff thrown in as a makeweight to get rid of it is being beamed in at the housewives and bedridden and unemployed and such like, the freaks who can't face going out in the daylight: acid trips, transvestites, urban guerillas, student revolutionaries, all manner of weirdness and sexual possibility in the midday darkness as we watch zonked with valium or serapax or flash-cured leaves from the barely-more-than-seedling dope plants, maybe there will be revolution yet. And Hoffman said, 'It's over, I feel so guilty, you let me be so free and I feel so guilty, I can't stand feeling so guilty.'

Is that why I don't phone this girl, is that why I play with the pendulum, try automatic writing, gaze at the harbour, stall, stall, stall, because I feel so guilty? Tonight my girlfriend's out somewhere, last week she was off at a party. 'Get to the reading later,' I said. 'Maybe,' she said. 'It'll probably go on late anyway. The party. So if you get a nice poetic groupie go ahead.' Even she talks as if these are poetry readings. Sometimes I'd add 'Prose and' to the 'Poetry Reading' signs. But everyone still calls them poetry readings. 'Liked your poem,' they say. Prose, you say, but you don't say, it sounds crazy, pedantic, who cares, poesis, creation, but you care. Prose.

A 747 roars overhead, one of the last ones out before the midnight refuellers' strike. The seagulls carry on their endless racket, squabbling or singing who knows, poetry reading maybe, we used to have readings in an old boatshed with the seagulls and the barges and the tugs drowning us out, sometimes.

You stand outside listening to the dynamo throb and the seagulls while the dope flash cures on the electric radiator. You say a prayer to be kept clear, to write this clear. You burp two, three times, the bad breath, the bad spirits expelled. You piss from the steps onto the garden below, you read somewhere Malayans piss outside at night to keep off evil spirits, these days you are glad to try any strategy, then you roll a smoke and light two more joss sticks.

Now a ferry goes by, cheers, whistles and weird cacophonous distorted music, its PA system dwarfed in the immensity of the dome of the night sky, the amplification of the reflecting harbour, the smoky clouds. The ships of fools, ergot-poisoned revelry, visions, gangrene, self-induced tortures. Its sound cuts out as it disappears behind the point and then it comes back again, in between gaps between the houses along the promontory. Two joints and maybe the two roaches and the fragments that weren't quite dried will make a third for a reward for when you're finished. Dope to get up, dope to come down, dope to work, dope to relax.

The first flying fox of the evening wafts by.

So maybe it isn't the girl, there is nothing about the girl, it is just the context, the prevailing circumstances. This is what it has come to, this is the absurdity, this is the paralysis, that the people who speak to you, the ones who are friendly, these are the ones you suspect: the people who smile, the people who agree, the people you like to be with. This is what has happened.

I am sitting in the car putting round a bit of psychic protection before setting off for the Coliseum Café where we do our readings. I have been watching this Greek movie about a writer who gets into what seem to be populist, leftist politics, and he's done over and broken by the security police who end up by running him. When later he becomes a sort of Leonard Cohen playing D.H. Lawrence leader they have it over him, everything is betrayal, everything is infiltrated. He is at the airport seeing off his wife, the ambassador's daughter, he married into power. She is leaving him for ever. And there is a terrorist with a bomb there as it happens, the usual airport scenario, and the writer talks the terrorist into switching off the bomb or whatever you do to stop bombs detonating. And then the security cop shoots the terrorist in the back. Dead. And I'm sitting in the car doing the closed eyes and muttered prayer bit when a voice speaks at my ear, I hurtle back into the present dimension, the face looming in at the window, did I achieve protection from the evening or did this make me jump out and was that intended, people not usually looming up at the car window at midnight, not even in my disordered world. It's the character from across the road, I don't know his name but we help start each other's cars once in a while. 'I dreamed about you last night,' he said, 'so I thought I'd bring the poetic outpourings of my soul and show you.' I figured he was going to ask me to read his poems, that is how I chose to interpret it, I said 'I'm doing a reading now,' assuming it was poetry, 'come along,' and they followed the car and they, he and his girlfriend, came into the café and I didn't see them after that. Nor did he ever bring his poetic outpourings for me to read, then or any other time.

I went through to the far end of the room where I recognised a poetic face or two, the place was full, so I find a corner to have a quiet smoke and to calm down. I get a seat at a table and look at the people there.

I look to see if I recognise anyone, I look to see if Joy's there, she had phoned in the afternoon to say she was coming, we rattled on for a while and that was when I noticed the familiar click back on the line, it had been away for two or three months. I thought, that will be interesting if she comes, 'why does she come over and visit you for two years if she doesn't want to fuck you?' my girlfriend said, and in the end, after two years, I was beginning to wonder. So two years ago you make a pass and she says this is a surprise and unexpected, which even then seemed a bit unpersuasively naive, so nothing happens, just embarrassment, sometimes she brings prawns or dope but never sex, so you don't worry, you talk and get stoned, once she gets you talking politics and her hands begin to shake and she rushes off to vomit, strange girl, you wonder why anyone would be bothered to keep on visiting for two years, you speculate on this, these days you have been forced to speculate on all your visitors, and the next week after you've been speculating out loud one evening she calls round and says, as she leaves, she wants to clear up a misunderstanding about something she'd said ages ago, not that she didn't find you attractive, oh no, but wanted to be able to keep on seeing you. And that was the last time you'd seen her, now she was working she conducted it all by phone and it still wasn't clear what was cleared up of the misunderstanding, there still remained some obscurities, it would be interesting to see her. And since she phoned up in the afternoon to see if I would be reading, I looked for her, but I couldn't see her. And another female person had phoned up from a municipal library to see if the reading was going to be on, and I assured her it was, but since I didn't know what she looked like I couldn't look for her. All this literary interest and my assurances that I will be there.

In this context, what hope is there for the girl who was there? At the time, of course, lots. It is only now, with the cicada on my leg, that I reassemble the context. And now I am ready to get to the girl I stop, make a pot of tea, roll the last very slender joint, and the cicada sits still, till I sit back down in the chair looking through the door to the harbour and it croaks once and moves from shin to thigh, did it walk or jump, I don't know, but it moved. When I get up to pour more tea it is restive so I entice if off with a *Time* subscription card dropped out of the paperback Balzac, it doesn't like the feel of it, can't get any purchase on the shiny surface, I carry it on the card and take it to the table and it wanders around among xeroxes of the 1892 *Worker,* then I carry it out to the step on an old Temple Library edition of Walton's *Lives* with an index card in it, 'Thank you for lending me this. XXXL'. Then it walks around a bit and leaves, and there is just the smoke of the last joss stick and the black harbour, the black sky, clouded over with bushfire smoke, no moon, just these bright lacquered blacks of the harbour, the lights glistening on the north shore, the double-decker line of light of the train going by along the cliff, the rumbles as a train crosses the harbour bridge, the sky a dustier, smokier black, all matt and flat, but the north shore pierced with white light, streetlights, a few yellow apartment lights, house lights, the greenish-white light of the naval moorings and the coal loader, a blotch of red and blue from a building sign, and the streaks from these light sources across the harbour to me in the doorway here.

Outside the cricket croaks derisively, a cockroach runs across the step, this is the stuff you write without the cicada, this is the signing off stuff, mood stuff, what you do after the script has ended, this is what you write when you want to write but don't want to write and you look at the view of the shimmering waters. Now water the plants and go to bed. Midnight. An empty ferry heads for the city.

After Magda the hooker and Minette the old-clothes-fashion boutique owner have gone, she is the most striking girl there. Luke has made a beeline for her. She is dark-haired, wearing red, sharing a bottle of spirits with another girl. I noticed her earlier, who is she with? I thought, what guy, but she seemed to be without a guy, she was drunk, her movements were those of someone out to wipe herself out, these are not unfamiliar movements at all, these are the movements we are quite familiar with, and she seemed to have reached the stage of drinking of looking for trouble, of waiting for someone to try and pick her up so that she could then yell and scream and maybe even swing a handbag or throw a glass or two, there is a certain familiarity about all this, maybe she was gay, there was a strong suggestion of a potential anti-man thing she and her friend had going. The friend was drunk too but she didn't have the air of being about to fall off the chair quite so much. There was an aura of aggression, of waiting to taunt.

Luke sits down with them and proceeds to roll a joint on the table, Mr Kool or Mr Krass, with the certainty of ensured protection or the stark insensibility of idiocy, but he's survived at it for a long time now. Rolling a joint can take a long time, if you lay it all out, gives your fingers something to do, eases you into a conversation, how can anyone tell you to fuck off when you're rolling them a smoke. And he always implies that it's you for whom the joint's rolled. He calls me over.

'This lady liked your piece,' he says.

'I didn't say anything about the piece. I said I liked him. Isn't he gorgeous?'

Luke raises his eyebrows and passes me the joint to light. He always preserves this old counter-cultural decorum, after you've rolled the joint give it to somebody else to light, accept this gracious gift. Other people light the joint they rolled themselves and puff and pull on it to get it started and sit there inhaling deeply, their eyes closed, slowly letting the smoke come out on their breath, maybe passing it down their nostrils, blowing smoke rings even, and half the joint's gone before they pass it on. Except for the smoke rings I belong to that category. But not Luke. So he raises his eyebrows and passes me the joint.

'Oh, now I've embarrassed him,' she says.

Her girlfriend howls. At least she seemed embarrassed too. An ecstasy of embarrassment.

'No, no,' I start to say, but I'm trying to hold my breath and not waste a puff.

'He's not used to this direct approach,' says Luke.

'I think he's smashing. I saw him standing up there and I thought, ooh la la, he's a bit of all right, didn't I?'

Her friend crunches up and splutters as if dug in the ribs.

'You're not so bad yourself,' I say. It doesn't sound very generous and it wasn't delivered with much breath. I try it again as 'You're pretty good yourself.'

It's hard to tell what's said and what's intended to be said but the intention evaporates, or what's heard, what's even listened to, a wickerwork of sounds.

'He's full of it, aren't you?' she says.

The aggression is there, it hovers around, but it's not in anything she says; everything she says is this flattering, friendly, warm, calculated, sexual note, you don't know quite what it is, it flits across all those categories, and somehow it carries the aggressive with it.

'Well,' says Luke, 'why don't you two sort out your arrangements together and we'll plan the rest of the evening.'

'No,' howls the friend. 'I've got to start early in the morning. I'm not going to be late again.'

'Well she can take him home and I'll get you up early in the morning,' he says.

'No you won't,' she says.

'Well, let's go back to my place for a drink, a smoke, watch a bit of TV, hear some good music . . .'

They disregard him, we all disregard him.

The café owner has finished clearing up, he stands there with a broom like he wants to fly off on it, we move outside to the footpath.

'Come back all of you to my place,' says Luke.

'Let's go somewhere, anyway,' I suggest, standing there on the early morning footpath.

'Oh, is that it?' she says. 'He thinks I'm going to take him home and fuck the pants off him,' she says to her friend, her friend jumps up and down in the road in rage.

'We can go to your place, we can go to my place. I don't mind,' I say, I'm so stoned, I won't sleep till dawn anyway.

'We've got a car,' the friend says.

So I follow them.

They end up in some back alley of an inner city suburb.

'A guy could get himself mugged following a couple of hoodlums like you into a dark alley like this,' I say.

They cackle.

What did we talk about? Clothes. 'You probably prefer faded jeans.' I shook my head, I didn't mind. If people are into clothes they're into clothes, I've no objections. But she was preoccupied with standing out, not fitting in. It was both, wanting to stand out, maybe not wanting to fit in there anyway, the café, but with years of uneasiness at not fitting in. 'You probably only like intellectuals. Straggly blonde hair and faded jeans.' I shook my head again.

'You didn't notice me,' she said.

'I noticed you,' I said.

'You didn't notice me watching you,' she said.

'No,' I said.

'How didn't you notice me undressing you?' she said.

Maybe I'd been so preoccupied with my own covert observation of the whole room, trying not to get caught in a fixed stoned stare at a face, that I hadn't noticed someone else's covert surveillance of me. But I hadn't, not even a flash of it.

Shyness, that was another topic. She'd been saying, 'He's shy, look how I've embarrassed him coming on so strong.' Now in the kitchen it's her turn to admit to shyness, or claim it.

'I don't believe you're shy,' she says. 'Are you really? You're as shy as me.'

She reads the tea leaves. 'Live till seventy-five. In a year to eighteen months I see you married with a child on the way. With the lady you're with, I'd say.'

'And you?'

79

'Me? Me, I'll be married with two boys and a girl.'

'Is that what you want?'

She gives an eldritch laugh. 'You don't believe all that, do you?' A cackle.

'I don't know,' I say.

'Oh, yeah,' she says. 'I've been doing it for years. But it has to be done with a pure spirit and a clean heart,' she says.

She says it like a talisman, like she's learned it off for a catechism.

'That's what my girlfriend says,' I say. It is exactly what she says, it hangs there with a disturbing resonance. These correspondences are what are disturbing these days. Once you would say, 'Yeah, yeah, exactly,' and rave on about kindred spirits. Now when someone sounds like a kindred spirit you wonder, when a phrase resonates with an amazing precision you tend to let it drift off, lose it in some conversational vagueness, practised diversion, escape routes on steep hills that bog you down in thick gravel if your brakes fail.

'You were bored silly at that café,' she says. 'I could see you, I was watching you.'

'I was just stoned.'

'You were bored. All those boring intellectuals. I don't blame you.'

'Well, some of it . . .'

'It was all boring and you know it,' she says.

She had been living with a guy and he went back to his wife, the wife didn't want him but when she found out he was living with her she played these games to get him back and now he's back with her, so now she was on her own again.

'What do you think I am?' she says. 'You don't think I go round picking up men in bars do you?'

'I don't know,' I say, absolutely truthfully, I don't know, and for all I know she might make her living picking up men in bars, she has that flamboyance, that swagger, that despising of men, or she might just be raging one night. She likes raging but she likes getting stuck into men, she and her friend mince men into pieces who try coming on strong.

'I thought you were either drunk or pilled out of your head.'

'Did you? Did we look like that? Did we?'

She's interested, cocks her head on one side evaluating that.

She lists the three pubs they'd been drinking in. 'And at the last one Ian knew you and so there we were at a fucking poetry reading.' They are the only three pubs I've drunk in during the past year, and why should they be talking with this person who knew who I was and then come on to the reading? She was dressed to drink at other places than those pubs though, more dressy, more the big hotel bars in the city, that tarty manner and that cold retreat from sexuality.

'I bought all this make-up stuff today, I bet the chicks you go for all have this nature stuff, no make-up.' She was right into it, facials, astringents, her eyes heavily mascara'd.

I move further in from the doorway, the wind off the harbour is too cool, I sit inside on the old worn couch but I leave the door open. The days have been passing as I wrote this. When I began I was writing to discover; now I have hardly any doubt. Before, when I began, it was a possibility I was having to drag up from the depths, didn't really want to know about it, yet it was there. It was there and not there. Now it is all too present. She talks about colours, the importance of colours for well-being, but this talk of the importance of colours, this is like the pure spirit and the clean heart, it is all too close to other conversations I have had at home. So is her talk about contraception, she'd just been to a doctor and he'd given her all this stuff on different sorts of contraception and this is another topic we've been exploring and discussing, another topic that is all too familiar, ordinary topics maybe, but too many ordinary topics and extraordinary coincidences, and more yet to come.

'You're as shy as I am, we'll never get anywhere like this,' she says, 'we'll be sitting here when dawn comes up,' she says, and stands up, she goes into the bedroom, 'put out the lights,' she says, and while I look round the kitchen for the light switch she has got into bed. 'That was quick.' 'I told you I'm shy,' she says. I sit on the bed and undress, this is the first time it's been clear we are going to bed, till now there's been the ambiguity, is she gay, is she games playing, is she prick teasing, this uncertainty that becomes a mystery, and like Tom Sawyer there I am, it was an adventure and it got him where he lived, and shouldn't I know about Tom Sawyer's adventures by now, but there is a softness, a gentleness in her eyes, and a slant in them, a cast, a fear, is this the flinch from the man, or is it the evil eye, the slightly smudged fearful look about the eyes, someone who's been treated badly, and my sentimentalism goes for it, the hurt, the wet shoulder, ever damp, the history it entails, a section into another world, why do the conversations always go so quickly to past loves, past sex, past doubtful episodes, is this the fantasy we really seek, not the fuck but all the past fucks of the other person's life, all their betrayals and lies and sufferings and explorations, exploitations, all the things that have happened to them sexually exchanged for all that we have ever done or had done to us? 'I'm not going to fuck you,' she says, we're in bed. 'All right,' I say, 'I'd like to, I'd rather fuck you than not fuck you, but that's all right.'

She lies there talking. Mostly she was this fragile kid who had been treated badly by men, every man had treated her badly, no details, no anecdotes, the odd pictures, used to be taken out and have to talk to these businessmen, she liked it when her boyfriend took her out and bought her a dress. Sometimes she seemed lost and gentle. Other times there was this hard, taught coldness. She mentions an expensive brothel in the city. 'Ever been there? Three hundred bucks a pop, isn't it?' 'I don't know. Seems a lot.' 'Oh, they're beautiful women, you know. All these businessmen.' The edge of contempt again. 'A friend of my boyfriend's had his girlfriend working there. I don't think that's right, do you?' 'I don't know,' I say, I don't know where she's at and I don't want to moralise about anyone, she might be talking about herself. 'Too lazy to work himself, I think that's off,' she says. 'You'll laugh if I tell you when I last fucked a guy,' she says, 'four or five months ago,' she says.

She has this thing about intellectuals. 'Everything I've been telling you is bullshit,' she says, 'I'm at university.' 'Where?' She says where. 'Doing what?' 'Staff,' she says, 'yeah, yeah,' she says, 'I've been kidding you, when I put my hair up I can be as straight as any intellectual.' She shows me, she pulls her hair up into a bun, holds it bunched there, profiled like a medallion. 'Funny,' she says, 'I seem to go for intellectuals, funny, the most unlikely men, I'm not at all intellectual,' she says, 'I read, I like reading.'

'You don't go around doing this a lot?' she says. There are different voices, this is a sudden voice that comes through. Some people's handwriting keeps changing within a letter, within a paragraph, the writing gets bigger, smaller, cursive, italic, backward sloping, forward sloping, straight, rounded, Van Gogh's was like that, so is this conversation, all over the place.

In the end we fuck. We kiss, I try to remember back about this, how passionate or unimpassioned, very stoned, she drunk or mandraxed or something, but we kissed on and off in this anonymous contact and we fucked, we pressed against each other and she took my prick into her and we fucked and then I think was all that stuff about not fucking about contraception so I ask does she want me to come out, but out of the blue, and whispered, these things are hard to catch, what? repeated, I can't hear her reply, I come out as I feel myself about to come, 'I've got an IUD,' she says, 'yuk,' she says, 'now it's all soggy,' 'Sorry,' I say, this is brilliant, this is ridiculous, I could see that rage surging up at this point but it doesn't, I feel I didn't do that very well, but maybe she's feeling that too, 'I'm a lousy lay,' she says, 'You're not,' 'No, I am, my boyfriend told me when he left,' she said, I look at her, there's a beauty there, a sad beauty amidst the blackness, this sadness, 'Why are you looking at me like that?' she says, 'Just looking,' looking at her, faces change so much, she doesn't like it, 'It makes me uncomfortable,' she says.

And we fuck again later, 'Have you come yet?' 'No,' I say, she asks again, lying there, very flat, very passive, 'Have you come yet?' 'No,' 'Why not?' You can take these things two ways, a challenge, a fear. 'Maybe because I'm enjoying making love,' I say, she smiles a bit, a moment, but she asks again, 'Maybe because I came already,' I say. I assume she needs assurance but that could be a male delusion, a male projection, but this lousy lay thing has hurt, that's the impression I get, or is this to make me feel the great saviour, rescuing mind and body, but I only think of that later.

She'd called me frightened. When we'd first got into bed she'd moved the shyness a stage, 'You're frightened, what are you frightened of?' The best way to unnerve anybody, tell them they're frightened. And what I must have been frightened was her, was she going to turn, that craziness in the eye, this is nothing weird or special, just that sudden turn, that hostility.

'You could be some Mata Hari,' I say.

She freezes momentarily, looks at me.

There are these things that sometimes we hear ourselves

84

saying. They drift by on the current of words and it is for us to listen to how meaningful they might be.

'You've got an answer for everything, haven't you?'

'Not everything,' I say.

'See,' she says, 'everything.'

She has been, 'Let's see,' she says, 'receptionist, model, typist, now I'm on a switch. How many words a minute can you type? Ten, twenty, forty, sixty?'

'Not sixty. Probably forty,' I say.

'Ah, we could get you a job,' she says. She laughs.

Somewhere she quotes Marvell, about love being parallel. 'That surprised you, quoting poetry,' she says. But it's not that, again it seems too researched, as if somebody has looked up what I've worked on, why should the only literary allusion I recall all evening be from someone I did a book on, maybe it's random, I've done other books on other people. But it disturbs me, I don't go back to it, I don't want to make it look like I'm expressing amazement that she can quote seventeenth-century poetry, I don't want to tell her what it is that really disturbs me, that it's like a scenario, another of these topics that will gel, but don't.

So there was this paranoia right through, but in these distinct moments, the rest of it wasn't like that, I just tried to notice things, isn't that why you enter into sexual adventures, voyages of exploration, instead of watching it on television you once in a while venture out into something and do it, and notice all the settings, to see how it compares, if it's authentic, or to see maybe if the television was authentic, reading it all carefully for a storehouse of memory, experience, unless you become so drunk it vanishes into oblivion, it was a nice dream but I can't remember a thing about it but I don't think it was a nightmare, was it?

I don't phone. She doesn't phone. The week passes and I go

to the Coliseum Café yet once more. She is there with a boy. They are wearing identical colours. Black. They look like they're in uniform. Paratroopers.

'You never phoned,' she says.

'Nor did you,' I say.

'What sort of week have you had?' she asks.

'Oh, you know,' I begin.

'*Three Days of the Condor*,' she says, answering for me.

One of the favourite movies for connoisseurs of paranoia, how to hide out when the CIA are out to get you.

She laughs.

It was about a year later she phoned up.

'You don't remember me,' she said.

'Yes, I do.'

'You didn't at first.'

One of these conversations.

'You said if I ever needed to, to phone you,' she said.

Did I? Could've. The old wet shoulder.

'I've been writing these things, I don't know if they're any good, I don't know how to write.'

'All you do is keep writing every day. That's the only way to learn how to write, nobody can tell you, it's just a question of keeping on doing it.'

'I was real crazy over you,' she said. 'Broke my heart,' she said.

It wasn't an easy phone conversation.

'Why don't you come and see me,' she said. 'I've got a new place.' She gave me the address. 'What are you doing now?'

'I was working,' I said. 'I'm pretty busy.'

'I bet you are,' she said.

There were silences. It didn't flow, the conversation.

'You know how I feel about this job I'm doing,' she said.

'I think so,' I said.

I was waiting for my girlfriend to come over, but she was late. I couldn't start cooking because she was buying what we needed on the way home. We were still together, not married, no child on the way. The tea leaves must have been wrong. Finally she rang.

'I'm picking up pizzas,' she said. 'The car wouldn't start and I had to wait ages for someone to come out and fix it.'

'What was wrong?'

'Nothing. The battery lead was loose.'

I grunted.

'They said somebody must have disconnected it.'

We sat on the front steps eating pizza and talking about the coincidence of the phone call and the disconnected battery lead while the seagulls squawked and the prawn trawlers trawled the harbour bed.

Smoke-oh

They sat there, the publisher, the cab driver, the librarian, the public servant, the scholar. We often sat around like this. Rolling up joint after joint after joint. Sometimes sitting there with the dealer with a great cardboard box full of lightly packed fragrant uncompressed heads. Sometimes with a block of Afghani on the brass table. Or it made the table brass, resonant, burnished in its presence. Cosy evenings as one more log was thrown on the fire, 'would you, please?' the fresh sharp smell of resin. 'Retsina,' says the philologist, licking a couple of papers, 'came from the resin seal they used when they kept wine in goatskin bags.' 'Goatskin bags,' we said. 'That's where the idea originated,' he said. We search for origins. 'The earliest dope reference is in Herodotus,' said the historian, 'he describes the Scythians putting the whole plant on the flames and then covering the fire and themselves with a blanket, and breathing in.' 'Sounds highly dangerous,' said the merchant seaman, 'what if the blanket caught fire?' 'It would be all right if it was made of hemp fibre,' said the dealer. 'I had a shirt made of it once,' said the orientalist. 'Even smoked the shirt off his back,' said the publisher. 'It makes good paper,' said the librarian, 'really nice paper, and it's much less destructive and polluting to the environment than making paper from timber. That really poisons the rivers, making paper from timber.' 'Be nice to have hemp rolling papers,' says the dealer. 'We could do a gift edition of

Leaves of Grass,' said the publisher. 'We could bind it in India,' said the orientalist, 'fill the binding with hash.' 'I learned book-binding in jail,' said the dealer. 'You'd have to lacquer it, otherwise the dogs smell it. They just put the dogs through the cargo.' 'They're real mean dogs,' said the public servant, 'they're junky dogs. They feed them heroin and then deprive them of it so they sniff it out.' 'Much like humans,' said the cab driver. The idea of junk-crazed or junk-deprived, strung out German shepherds does not turn us on. 'We could use heat-seal plastic,' says the publisher. 'Like records,' says the public servant. 'Like books,' says the writer. But these are just pipe dreams. Hemp seeds of the imagination. Armchair smuggling scams. 'We're not out of papers are we?' Pairs of hands start feeling simultaneously through pockets, wriggling in chairs. 'I wish you could buy them in the supermarket,' says the academic. 'In bulk.' 'Would that be any cheaper?' says the public servant. 'Probably. But you could get a dozen packets at a time instead of having to go up to the corner store all the time.' 'They get to know you,' said the librarian, 'they smile in that funny way, "Something else?".' 'You get milk and bread and eggs and tomatoes,' says the publisher, 'and, oh, a couple of packets of papers.' Mixed business. 'You can buy rolling tobacco with them,' says the cab driver. 'Not if you're trying to give up,' says the philologist. 'Anyway your consumption of papers is far in excess of your tobacco consumption,' says the public servant. 'I buy them at different places,' says the merchant seaman, 'wherever I go I get a couple of packets, just so I'm not always going to the corner shop.' 'The corner shop is how they get you,' says the publisher, 'they remember all these things, most of them are all right but you might get some full-on fascist falangist who'd dob you in.' 'Anyway, they know,' says the public servant, 'they may be all right but the point is they know. They look at you.'

'All those street kiosks are a surveillance network,' says the cab driver, 'those guys have to work with the cops, whenever they're looking for someone they're the first people they go to.' 'If you sold them in tens in two-dollar packs,' says the public servant, 'they'd be like a packet of cigarettes.' 'Those Spanish papers are really neat,' says the merchant seaman. 'Maybe we could import them cheap,' says the scholar, 'Mexico.' 'China,' says the librarian. 'Rice paper would be something,' says the public servant, 'healthier than this stuff.' 'What is this stuff?' We don't know. 'They used to make paper out of plague rags,' says the historian. 'There's a duty on imported paper but not on printed paper,' says the publisher. 'So we'd print something on each paper,' says the merchant seaman, 'I reckon an economy style pack. Bulk buy through supermarkets.' 'Do supermarkets sell them?' 'They keep them locked in the till. It means you have to ask for them and they can check you out.' 'Maybe they want it like that.' 'Maybe they do, but think of the money in bulk papers.' Money talks. We could include filters in the pack. We could have a simple economy pack and a deluxe pack with filters. We'd make a fortune. We look at the local rolling papers. Anything made locally could be made cheaper somewhere else. We could supply cheaper than these. Healthy gums, no inking, no dyes; we could investigate glues. We'd only be taking on one or other of the largest multinationals of the oligarchy. We forget who makes the local rolling papers but we know it's owned by one of the multinational giants. Most things are. We have such good ideas but so little likelihood of implementing them. We are pretty well surplus to requirements, marginal men, old tea-heads of yet another lost generation, watching it all go up in smoke.

The Wrath of Farmers

Returning to my home town again in my mind, preparatory to returning again in my body, I find not unpredictably or indeed unexpectedly that I hold off. Is it that having explored it already, thought about it so much when I lived there and knew nowhere else, I have written all I would ever want to write, having recalled all I would ever want to record? Or is it that there are unrecorded but not unrecallable episodes, things I should yet look into? The old familiar tautening of the stomach muscles. But the stabs and jabs of pain, are they just the splinters from scraping the barrel and a sign it's time to move on, but I have moved on, now I've moved back? Or are these the jabs of pain and tenderness of the as yet unrecorded episodes of trauma and angst and ill-repressed horror? Of course I could return looking for happy stories, comic stories, and then it would just be the pain of laughing.

Mushrooms were our last link with Germanic communality. The shared landholdings had gone, the common lands had been enclosed, now we had no land. But my father still persisted in some of the old ways. We still collected firewood, blackberries, horse manure. The horse manure mixed with water and turned into liquid manure fed the garden that produced pretty well all our vegetables. But some things were still untamed, shy, elusive. You had to look for mushrooms, they were not something you could cultivate. There were fields where mushrooms could be expected to be found year after year, and then one year there wouldn't be any, or one year the field would be ploughed and the pasture buried. Then sometimes they would appear in a new field, or a field returned to pasture after years of having been ploughed, and with horses grazing it it would produce mushrooms. Whenever you found them you picked them, great big field mushrooms the size of dinner plates, that was the phrase that was always used. Of course when they were fried they shrunk down in size. Fried with bacon for breakfast. They were best found early morning and when my father discovered them growing in a field only a field away from where we lived, he would get up early on a weekend morning to pick them. I can't remember now whether it was a Saturday or a Sunday morning. 'The old lady who gathered sticks on a Sunday went up into the moon,' my Aunt told me. Sitting in front of the fire I'd been gathering sticks for that day, Sunday, just this year. How could I ever have forgotten? But I'd managed to. By living in a country where you don't have fires. Don't have fireplaces. Wouldn't mind a fire in winter once in a while.

The early morning meadows at the edge of town, the sun on them like folds of warm soft glowing blanket, transparent and sucking up the morning dew. Amidst the cowpats and horsepats the fresh surprised mushrooms. We only ever ate field mushrooms, the rest were held to be poisonous, and many were.

There was a farmer's house overlooking the field, an urban-looking raw, red brick, two-storey villa with blank red walls like a fortress, like the end of a terrace. This year it is empty, boarded up, uninhabitable because it has no mains water, sewer, or power. Next year no doubt it will be renovated. But at this time of the mushrooms they lived there, the farmer and his wife, with pump water, a wood burning range, and oil light. They would have lived by the seasons, by the light.

Every day, even Sundays, he would be up in those beautiful fresh fragrant mornings, shaving at the window, looking across his fields.

'No, no,' said Dad, 'I would never have gone on a Sunday morning. That was the terrible thing, you see,' he said, chuckling.

He'd walked home from church with a friend who was a sidesman. Sidesmen handed out and collected the prayer books and hymn books when you went in and out of church and took the collection, passing the big wooden plate with the green felt base so the money put in didn't jingle, passing the plate from row to row down the church, standing at the end of each row of pews watching it progress, policing it no doubt so nobody palmed a few coins back into their hand instead of giving, could there have been such dark suspicions? I'm sure there could. The friend was lamenting the good old days when you could find field mushrooms, and my father told him where there were some growing.

'I never expected he would go on a Sunday,' Dad said. 'Fancy that, a sidesman.'

He'd taken a bag and he'd half filled it when there was an awful confrontation. An enraged farmer, with a shotgun, berating him.

'And I've seen you here every weekend.'

'No you haven't, I've never come before.'

'I've seen you. Don't you bloody tell me no lies. I'll call the bloody police. And if you try to move I'll bloody shoot you too. Every bloody weekend I've seen you. And a bloody Sunday too. And you a bloody sidesman. Wait till I seen the vicar. I've been waiting for you. I knew as I'd catch you eventually. Never expected to catch a sidesman, though. Wait till I seen the vicar.'

Not that there was much likelihood of that. He was one of

the heathen, I think, that farmer. There was a lot of heath country, houses scattered their distance from each other, not clustered together round a church.

'Though,' said Dad, 'you can see why people stay heathens when they see the way respectable churchgoing sidesmen behave.'

Later he got baptized and confirmed and became a sidesman himself. And we'd pretty well stopped going for mushrooms by then. It was getting too risky. Once you've encountered the wrath of a farmer you're pretty heavily traumatised. This was only wrath encountered by proxy. But when you've encountered the authentic wrath, even the tale of the proxy resonates.

Across the road from where we lived were fields where cabbages and peas and potatoes were grown. Occasionally we would have to go in there to retrieve a ball we'd thrown or kicked over the railings. But generally we kept out. There was little enough enticing, anyway. Once, however, we investigated some glass cloches. We were examining what was in them when there was a shout from down the hill, where the field sloped into the withies along a stream. It was like a scarecrow come to life, the featureless old flapping jacket and floppy hat gesticulating and calling out and, we soon realised, coming towards us. We ran. The shout of a farmer is an ugly shout. The sort to turn your bowels to water. That is its intent. Not even a farmer enraged. Just a farmer, a regular, typical farmer's shout has enough rage, they are in perpetual rage against the public and the city and government and nature and small boys. Maybe the chemical companies keep them sedated now, maybe the superphosphates and the weed-killers and insecticides gently narcotise them. I don't know. I've kept well away from farmers since this moment of terror as we heard the bloodcurdling 'Oi', the Bacchic 'io' of rejoicing reversed into this trumpeting of trouble, and saw him pounding up the slope between the rows of peas, and we dropped the cloches and ran, ran out of the field, over the railing, down the road past half a dozen houses, up the gap between the houses to the field at the back, and then my partner in crime went his way right and I went my way left, past the backs of the houses, then over the back fence, down the garden path, through the back door and up the stairs into my bedroom and a quickly locked door. And the farmer pounding after me, past the astonished neighbours gardening in the mid-morning weekend, past the scents of fresh peas and freshly chopped mint sauce wafting along the garden paths, over the back fence, our back fence, and down to where Dad stood.

'Had me worried,' said Dad. 'I thought he was going to have a heart attack. Shouldn't be running around like that at his age.'

And upstairs, panting on the bed, I lay like all those movie protagonists I was yet to see who've climbed a staircase only to find a grille at the top. I just hoped they didn't let him in. I was horrified that he'd followed me into the garden. I thought I might have given him the slip. Or the fence might have restrained him. A social taboo. For all the fuss farmers make of fences, it's amazing how little respect they show for anybody else's.

I can't remember whether I might have had a few pea shells in my pocket, fresh young peas eaten from the pod being very succulent. I guess I could have. Nor can I remember how Dad saved me. but saved I was. No-one dragged me out of the bedroom that I can recall. This is probably one of the incidents I don't want to remember. What I do remember are the important things, like keep well away from farmers, and make sure there are no farmers around when you go in a field, always look to see whether they mightn't be bent double and out of your line of vision, or wielding their cut-throat razor in the bathroom window overlooking the field you're in.

95

Three Incidents for
a Mercia Quartet

I can remember the incident now. And anything remembered so long it's fair to suspect carries some unrevealed meaning. Perhaps it was our last sixth form party or the first old boys' dinner. Something rather formal in the school hall, the benefactor looking down on us from his portrait high on the wall, feet spread apart on that tiger skin. All males, all-male school. And here were these token females from the girls' school. And I was talking to Marian who was pale and interesting and artistic, about *The Alexandria Quartet,* that burst of the exotic into our dutiful pursuit of English literature, modern fiction, good books. The light, polished wooden panels attended Marian admiring the bravery of one of our titled actors for being homosexual. And I was wafting off turning this small town into Alexandria, featuring the exotic eye-shadowed girlfriend of a class mate of mine; he drove her around in a three-wheeler Morgan runabout. What fantasies I could weave about her. There were locales as bleak as any duck shoot you could imagine, up river where the island was, and all round water meadows and wildfowl, the island where the citizens hid out after flaying a couple of Danish tax-gatherers alive, and the skin is still there in a display case in the cathedral. The exotica tripped readily off the inner pen. The best books, the evanescent never written ones, unheard melodies. It had got to me, that landscape of desire, and I knew it wasn't Alexandria I was to go to because that was written now and I knew it wasn't just a matter of turning this small town into some pornotropica, it was finding somewhere else.

The other incident was just Marian and me and our bicycles, those inflexible intrusions from the world of the absurd that we had yet to discover and find we had lived. A gravelled driveway up to a country house, past a row of civil defence sheds. Cover your windows with white of egg and sit under the table. It had an almost religious simplicity this advice on how to survive man's greatest technological triumph of destruction yet. Greatest that we knew of, anyway. Later we began to realise there were many worse things than we were aware of.

If our bicycles came between us, no less did our navy gaberdine raincoats or our plastic yellow cycling capes. We stood, we talked. I didn't want to do the wrong thing and offend, did nothing which maybe offended more than anything, and yet there again maybe didn't. These sites of adolescent anxiety, why revisit them?

And the third and final episode, with me in the driveway between our house and next door, a drafty passage just wide enough to get a car down to the garage, and against those wooden creosoted doors between the whitewashed stuccoed walls I'm practising tennis, could it be, belting the ball against the garage doors, the sort of thing to drive everyone mad. And I'm only doing it out of a forlorn and wretched sense of duty, something expected of me, isn't that what it was, make a man of you, good at games, etc. And Marian and her parents pass by on a walk. My parents must have been there too, gardening at the front of the house. Brief dialogue. And me, silent as the grave etc. She wrote me a note: Why?

Because, you see, her grandfather had been the hated foreman, the loathed and detested bane of my father's and his father's life. What could I do? Admit to dating the foreman's granddaughter? And it wasn't even that strong a class line, not like I would have liked it to have been to understand it later. There was a detestation apart from the foreman's role, whereas Dad had always liked the boss's son who killed himself when the place began to fail, and Dad always said that it was unreasonable pricing by some of the men that led to the collapse that caused all that, and it was one of the things that deeply saddened him.

Lonely boys belting tennis balls at walls and doors, windy grey weekends, green drainpipes with loops of old greyed string where lines had once been strung and broken, sad grey manhole covers and pale concrete, and sparrows twittering from the roof gutters. And maybe the hope of once in a while an interesting aircraft overhead.

NY 1969

Jon and Nora lived on Riverside Drive though the windows looked over an intersecting street, not onto the river. The apartment door had three locks and someone had been mugged in the elevator three weeks earlier. There was a big poster of Eldridge Cleaver in the hallway of their apartment. Eldridge Welcome Here, it said. This was after he skipped bail and was in Algeria or somewhere. They rolled a couple of joints.

'Getting stoned?' they said.

'I don't think so,' I said.

'It takes a while to get used to it,' they said. 'The first two or three times we didn't get stoned either.'

Seemed strange to me. Another illusion.

We went down to dig the car out of the snow that had piled up around it. The snow was fifteen feet deep. Caverns of snow. And a tiny Fiat 500 lost amidst it. Snow ploughs swept the streets clear and pushed the snow towards the pavements burying parked cars. Especially little European ones. We had shovels and dug. It seemed hilarious. I had to lean on the spade while I laughed.

'He's stoned,' said Nora.

We went to a Janis Joplin concert.

'She's got a new band,' they said.

We stood in line outside the Filmore East. Uniformed police stood on the sidewalk and the dealers called out 'Get your acid before you go in' walking up and down the lines.

We sat high up in the roof, sharing another joint. The ushers walked up and down the aisles with flashlights calling out 'No smoking'. No-one took any notice of them and they took no notice of anyone. They had a girl along from one of those expensive, exclusive women's colleges. 'You're not really into it, are you?' she said, 'I can see you're not really into it.'

About seven o'clock one morning there was a knocking at the door and then it was answered and then there was some talking in the corridor beside the Eldridge Welcome Here poster and then the men's voices stopped and the door closed and Nora came into the spare room where I was just lying in bed, figuring that was the best thing to do, just lie there, possibly with the sheet over my head.

'Don't freak,' she said. 'The pigs have just taken Jon away.'

The university had served a private writ for disorderly behaviour and attempted petty larceny. He'd jumped on the chairman's table in the middle of the disciplinary proceedings after the occupation, and tried to grab the chairman's gavel so the proceedings couldn't go on.

'They've taken him to the tombs,' she said. 'You better get dressed and we'll go and bail him out. Get yourself some breakfast while I phone my mother.'

We went down to the Central Courts and borrowed a lawyer from the Black Panther trial going on there at the same time. We sat in the courtroom as a succession of hookers came up before the whatever legal figure it was they came up before, and waited for Jon's turn. Outside the courtroom in the corridors there were armed police everywhere. We tried to talk to a lawyer Nora was borrowing for a moment, and the cops came along and said 'Break it up.' Every time more than two people stood together, they came and broke it up. This wasn't long after a bunch of cops out of uniform suddenly appeared in the corridors and attacked a whole bunch of Black Panthers on trial there.

Maybe they weren't in uniform because they were off duty.

Now cops in cop uniform and Panthers in Panther uniform, dark shirts, berets, watched everything.

Nora's mother drove us back. Jon said it had been quite interesting being in the cell with all the hookers. Nora's mother insisted on a scenic drive. Nora complained but her mother said since I'd never been to New York before somebody had to show me it. The United Nations. Flags flying. Those sort of things. The United Nations is the only one I remember.

One day we went to Ocean Hills Brownsville. It used to be a Jewish area, now it was a Black area. Jon was writing the words and this other person was doing the photographs, it was to be documentary photo-journalism about the teachers' strike and racism and poverty.

We went inside a school. One of those P.S. and three digit schools. Not Saint Somebody or Other's. The classes seemed small and the kids just seemed to run around and talk and play around all the time. It seemed like chaos.

Afterwards we went across to a milk bar and Jon had his tape-recorder on and started talking to people there and then the store-owner got mad at him asking all these questions, 'Why are you asking all these questions, you come snooping round here and I don't like it, that tape-recorder, I don't like it.'

He said, 'It's worse than Viet Nam here, man. At least they can get supplies. The trucks won't come in here, man, the kids take off the wheels and steal all the stuff, they won't make deliveries, we can't even get supplies here, at least they get supplies in Viet Nam.'

Jon and Nora took me to a party. It was SDS from Columbia and Black Panther supporters. This was the time the PL were splitting the SDS with their hard line and anti-drug line. Students for a Democratic Society and the Progressive League. This was the first time the radical white and radical black had had a party together for nine months. There was an immense wariness. I talked to a black girl from Pittsburgh about the English class system and the sufferings of the English working class. And the dope went round in a hookah. Generally the whites talked to the whites and the blacks talked to the blacks. There were movies being shown of the Columbia occupation. People looking to see themselves or each other. Stars. Some covering their faces, turning away. Nora set about organising the 'Free Jon' campaign. When they left I went with them. They offered me the keys and told me how to operate them, turn the first to the right, turn the second one and a quarter times to the right, turn the third one . . . And I knew I'd never be able to do it and I'd have to wake them up in the middle of the night. So I went home with them. We smoked some more dope and looked at Zap comix and listened to 'John Wesley Harding'.

Pity the poor immigrant who wishes he'd stayed at home.

We went to the Village to a re-run movie house and saw *Ninotchka*. The first time I saw Garbo. And we saw *The President's Analyst* and *Skidoo*. I went to whatever it was art museum and saw 'Guernica'. This was when the Americans were bombing Vietnam. I read an article about how Marilyn Monroe had had an affair with John F. Kennedy and how LBJ had fucked the bullet wound in JFK's neck when the body was flown back from Dallas. I had trouble ordering coffee because of the American way of pronouncing it. 'Why don't you bring your typewriter in next time,' the man behind the counter said. We went to a famous delicatessen festooned with salami. A banner was strung across a wall. SEND A SALAMI TO YOUR BOY IN THE ARMY.

Jon took me up to the campus where he taught. It was all suburban out there. A girl came into his room and said she was the reincarnation of J.S. Bach. He introduced me to a man in the corridor whose name he blocked on, he couldn't remember it suddenly in the very act of introducing me to this person, who was the chairman of the department, the heaviest of the professors, and a poet too, an international name, who would expect to be known. Jon stood there gesturing with his arm towards the person, going, 'er, er,' and this person assumed that it was deliberate, that it was a mocking of the pretensions of authority and celebrity, in keeping with Jon's expected behaviour given his political stance.

'No, no,' Jon said, 'I had a complete mental block.'

We met two poets on the faculty, mid-western poets, very cynical about the literary machine, very ambitious, but dour. We sat in a roadhouse bar decked out to look like a pioneering western hut, very bare.

I went to the first enrolment for Jon's class in 'Literature and Sexuality'. He had another course on 'Literature and Revolution'. He taught *The Story of O* and *Heart of Darkness* and *Fanny Hill* and Mao Zedung.

I caught a flight to Texas and talked to the girl in the seat beside me. She was met at the airport by her boyfriend and they offered me a lift to the address I was going to. On the way we got pulled over by a cop. 'I've seen you around,' the cop said. He booked him for having a faulty muffler. They dropped me off at the house. There was a party going on. 'Come on in,' said the people I was staying with, but they just dropped me off.

Pioneers

Santa Teresa, what do we remember of you, besides walking along the waterfront and avoiding the panhandlers who came out of the bushes in the late afternoon and slept on the beaches until the police moved them off in the early hours of the morning, young men, young men looking like old men, and men approaching old age, Vietnam veterans for the most part, who killed and defoliated and supplied and backed up 'for their country's good' and came back narcotised, chemically saturated, spaced out, superfluous, 'Mister, can you spare a dime,' they don't say that any more but what they do say we rush on past so we don't have to hear, our only impressions are from old movies, old songs, old cartoons, the present is too painful, they ask for change but we don't hang around to capture the idiom or to give them any.

And along the bicycle track along the waterfront the tourists rode their bicycles and their pedal carts, and beside them the really keep-fit ones ran or jogged, wired up to the rhythmic beat through the earphones clamped to their heads, or others strapped up to roller skates at their feet, following the lure of perpetual motion, perpetual health, perpetual youth, whoosh whoosh whoosh, this is life, this is activity, this is what we do to know that we are really doing it, that we are, that we exist, that we are more palpable than the wisps of sea fog condensing from the cold current and the hot air, shrouding the coast in a damp, still deathliness that seeped into the cavities of your bones and the deep recesses of your consciousness and sucked you into suicide in the stories of the creative writing classes. While all night long the foghorn sounded at the end of the wharf. 'Where is he?' Lydia wanted to know, 'where does he sit pressing that button all night long, how does he know when to stop, who tells him when to start?'

'Ask the palm reader on the wharf,' I suggest.

'You do not need to come here,' says the palm reader, 'you can already tell these things.'

We walk down the length of the wharf and back at night with the holidaymakers and tourists and other aimless ones, one night a sea lion sticks his head up and looks at us and goes away again, 'Ah, old Grandad,' the locals tell us, they know him, he lives there, they know him better than they know each other, at least they know his name. Now we know his name.

Sometimes we sniff familiar wisps of cannabis but mainly we sniff the smell of fish, cooking and rotting, from the restaurants on the wharf, and hurry past the counters with their tanks of dying lobsters and crabs, out to the end of the wharf where men and their sons and men alone and sons and daughters alone sit with their nylon lines to catch the fish that have cruised in close to the wharf to eat the fish scraps thrown into the sea. There are also candy shops and ice cream parlours but generally we have already eaten when we come down to the wharf, and we just walk its length and back again and then go back aimlessly home, which is what we call the place where we are living, and wonder why we are living here and what sort of life there is here to live. The palm trees stand distinctively along the waterfront and tell us nothing. Sometimes we buy a newspaper from the vending machines on the sidewalk, and it tells us equally little and we are equally unsurprised.

Where are the stories? Where is the narrative, where are

the threads that explain how things happen, or does nothing every happen? The first policeman to be shot and wounded in Santa Teresa for thirteen years is shot and wounded in the new year. A quiet little town, a tight little town, tight little quiet little towns with so little violence are not necessarily all their record might proclaim. The dialectic of suspicion suggests that all that the record shows is that it's all sewn up. 'They hush it up,' says the lady on the shuttle bus from the airport. 'There's a lot of street violence, stabbings and muggings and rapes, but they keep it out of the papers because it's bad for tourism.' But it's not the street violence that we speculate about. We look up from the wharf at the rich houses in the hills. Is there a smell of wealth distinct from the smell of crime? Are our senses not acute enough, so we fail to distinguish what might be distinguishable? All property is theft; but do different sorts of theft exude a different scent? What generated your wealth Santa Teresa, where the biggest employer is the county and the next biggest is the university, or is it the other way round, but doesn't it either way round make the same point?

'It's half way between Mexico and Haight Ashbury,' says Col.

Thanks be that somebody smokes here. Even if we have to wait till the end of the party when everybody has gone home except us, and then Col disappears and we wonder if he has packed in the party too but he comes back with a joint, ready rolled, no stash brought out on display, this isn't the sixties any more, not by a quarter of a century, can so many years have gone by in a flash when they seem to drag so now and hang heavy on us? One drag, two drags, at last, it seemed like it would never happen and this is California.

'These young guys were like pioneers,' Col says. 'They were tough. They were like marines. They believed in adventure. They trekked over mountain passes with back-packs. They went untrodden ways. They could handle themselves. Their hands were lethal weapons. They exercised. They did training. Up and down the beach. Up and down the hills. Packs on their back. They made sure they were fit. And only the fittest survived. And they brought it in. They were the conquistadors of the modern age.'

Col's wife takes a puff but refuses any more. Lydia refuses it altogether. I am relieved. It's only one joint. Col produces a roach clip so we can smoke it down till our lips scorch without burning our fingers.

'Then they got corrupted. They got greedy. They still believed in it. But it was no longer a pure cause. Now they were into making money from it. They stopped relying on their hands and they started carrying guns. They gave up the mountain passes and stuffed it under automobile seats and into dummy gas cans. They gave up on training and took to bribing. They got into real estate. They got into buying and selling generally. That became their drug. Money. Wealth. Building regulations. Redevelopment. Bribing city hall. It became a business. The age of the pioneers was gone. They became like their fathers.'

'Maybe they were always like their fathers,' said Lydia.

'No, these were good kids, these were idealists. They thought it should be available so they brought it in.'

'But who financed them in the first place?' Lydia said. 'Where did they get the cash in the first place to buy in bulk? Doesn't that suggest they were just doing their parents' business, just branching out from army surplus and real estate into dope and back out again into real estate and selling army surplus aircraft to the big growers?'

'No,' said Col.

'She's got a point,' said Victoria.

'No,' said Col. 'These were idealists, they believed in what they were doing.'

'So did their fathers,' said Victoria.

The roach has gone out.

'Maybe they were just set up,' I chip in. 'Maybe their idealism was observed and exploited. They went in blind with their parents' cash, and were monitored all the way along. They made the contacts their parents' generation could never have made, and once the contact was secure and the markets were established, then the normal imperatives of big business could operate and their parents took them in as partners. Even when we think we are free we are being monitored. Our freedom is the dynamic that motivates us, that powers us to make the contacts and extend the network for the people who've always been controlling us, parents, big brother, Uncle Sam.'

'I think we've got a radical here,' says Col. 'How did you get here? I thought they'd cleaned people like you right out.'

'It worried me too,' I said. 'I thought maybe they'd brought me over to assassinate me.'

In the mornings the woodpecker would wake us up, tapping out sharp bursts of rhythm on the telegraph posts. All the way up the posts the woodpeckers had drilled holes; now for variety they sat on top of the plastic junction boxes and beat on them. This way they got a succession of different pitches. At first we thought they were mechanical hammers, part of the ceaseless daily mechanical sounds, the back-pack with its motor to suck up leaves, the motorised lawn edge-trimmer, the lawn mowing services that manicured the lawns, every house on a different day, the branch and hedge trimmers, the vacuum cleaners, the eternal throb of the washing machines and dryers, the coastguard helicopters, the presidential helicopters, the highway patrol helicopters, the hammering and sawing as the timber frame houses were extended, decks built out, storeys built up. But it was organic life that greeted us first thing in the morning, a small striped speck of such, beating out its aubade beneath the silver fog cover, making a clatter that even the mocking bird couldn't imitate that imitated every other cry and sang all night, its repertoire so extensive.

The writers' group met in town for lunch. I said I'd wait till I felt strong enough. 'No, no, there are no heavy drinkers there, not now,' said Col. I still delayed. But Col was telling the truth. They met at twelve and had gone by two. This was not a society where you got drunk and wiped out the afternoon. On campus no-one even seemed to have a drink midday, except those who'd started at breakfast and gone home for lunch.

They wrote books about sailing across the Pacific and about how to service your Mercedes-Benz and about sex, jealousy and marriage and about bullfighting and about fighting alcoholism, and thrillers. There were a lot of crime writers in Santa Teresa.

'Now those guys know what they want,' said Col. 'They have no existential doubts. They know what writing's about. Money.'

He passed the joint across.

And on campus? Did they know what writing was about there?

They couldn't bring themselves to talk about it. There is no dialogue for this. Their thoughts had worn themselves into too deep a groove. It bored even themselves, let alone Lydia and Victoria. It took them too deep down into the mire and they would get bogged there and crushed beneath some passing cart, broken on the wheel.

One bit of dialogue.

I had borrowed Col's last novel from the campus library. The last one to be published, published way back now, seventeen years back.

'I liked it, I liked it a lot.'

'Thank you,' said Col.

The necessary punctuation of sucking on a joint.

'That was the grave of my literary career.'

'I enjoyed the one about Santa Teresa, too,' I said. About the movement. About when the bank was burned down in the heady sixties and seventies.

'Ah yes,' said Col. 'If the novel was the grave of my literary career, that little polemic was its tombstone.'

Now the bank had pretty well burned itself down.

What they said on campus was you could take Col out of the Haight but you couldn't take the Haight out of Col.

Blacklists no-one mentioned. Only Victoria said that to Lydia over lunch one day.

This was a free society and here was the furthest West of freedom. Too far from the literary East perhaps.

'But you and I,' said Col, 'we made our choice, we rejected that metropolitan literary world. We could see the destructions of that game.'

It was the other destructions we hadn't seen. Not then.

Down at the writers' lunch one of the thriller writers lent me a current issue of a literary quarterly with a new story by Col. It was about a lone man with a gun who takes a small child hostage and holes up in an apartment and shoots it out with the police. They kill him.

Hanging Out

In the late afternoon they drove down to the beach and parked and sat and looked at the waves and at people flying kites and at dogs chasing seagulls and at the endless joggers.

'How long does it take you to walk to the beach from your place?' Col asked.

'It wouldn't take long,' Marcus said.

'How long?'

'Oh, I don't know, maybe fifteen minutes, twenty minutes.'

'Have you done it?'

'What, walked? No, not yet.' This was California, they'd hired a car, why would they walk? But there again this was California, the land of the eternally youthfully healthful.

'In Atlantean times,' said Lydia, 'there was an incarnation of souls who got totally into movement. They just liked to run and jump and fly and see themselves doing it. They were into being eternally young and eternally physical and they never developed any other consciousness so they were doomed to be reincarnated till they understood the meaning of life.'

'I'm glad the meaning of life isn't running and jumping and flying,' said Marcus.

'No, it's not,' said Lydia.

'What happened to them?' he asked.

'They kept getting reincarnated. This last time they were reincarnated as Californians.'

'Let us take you to our club,' Victoria, Col's wife, said. 'We can walk there.'

They did and she showed them the swimming pools and the tennis courts and the squash courts and the machines.

Marcus couldn't bear to look at them.

'How can you be a writer and not bear to look at things?'

'Easily,' he said.

'Yes, but you can't bear to look at things writers write about.'

'I know,' he said. 'I can't bear to write, either. Not about those things. Not about lots of things.'

'Try,' said Lydia.

They were awful things.

'In their previous incarnation the people who designed these would have made torture chambers,' Lydia said.

There were things you sat on and held onto and had to push with your arms and legs, things that looked like they would push you and tug you and stretch you and rack you. There were weights to weight-lift and punch-bags to punch. It was all black leather and polished chromium, or simulated black leather, and people in shorts and singlets pushing and puffing and exerting themselves, straining against these calculated weights and forces and stresses and tensions. And polished floors. And locker rooms.

It was like the gym at school. It was a gym.

'That was something else I never wrote about,' Marcus said. 'Walking the horizontal beam, I was terrified. Hanging from the wall ladders I was paralysed with fear. Leaping the wooden horse, I was petrified. somersaults. Rope climbing. I think I was tortured in a previous incarnation in one of these places. When they were used as torture chambers. Before they pretended it was for recreation. That was torture enough.'

He couldn't wait to get outside, even sitting between the

wire mesh of the tennis courts and the blue vacuity of the swimming pool was better.

'You come here at weekends?' he said.

And evenings. Afternoons sometimes.

Of course torture could be looked at in a positive light, like everything else. The evil that is done to you can be turned to a good in developing your consciousness. The tortures you suffer may help bring you enlightenment, looked at in an enlightened way. How can you hate the hand that betrays you, for that betrayal is an enlightenment, it reveals the truths you had blindly refused to see, now you know better how the world is, now you have a deeper perception of how things are done.

Give me scopolamine, give me acid, give me spatial distortion and consciousness disorientations. One man's poison is another man's recreation. The fingernails ripped off, the eyes put out, the electrodes to the genitals, the push from the high building, please no. Some people remembered meeting beneath the pyramids. Marcus didn't. But those physical fears were imprinted deep enough to be a memory of something. The gym stirred up something. But the chemical and herbal substances, he had come to accommodate them, love them even. Never mind that acid was evolved as a truth drug by the CIA, never mind that the FBI used marijuana to get people to talk, these were the poisons you got to love, got to desire, got to be dependent on.

'Down the east end of the beach,' he said, 'let's drive down there.'

Forget the heavy trip about walking there. Or jogging there. Let's cruise down in this great American hire car. And hang out.

This was where people gathered in little clusters on the beach gazing into the sunset and shivering and sitting gazing fixedly for long periods of time. This was where they rolled their own smokes and passed them across to each other. This end of the beach had that ambience. Not the ambience of the homeless who crawled out at twilight and sat there drinking port wine till they got sleepy enough to sleep till the cops came and woke them up and moved them on. Nor the ambience of the aerobic jogging puffing clean-shorted head-banded blond and beautiful young couples, I can do it I can do it I'm not sick I'm not flabby I'm as healthy fit and beautiful as you are don't leave me don't abandon me don't desert me for some brighter blonder whiter-shorted blanker-eyed jogger, I'm not going to give up and stay back home and eat corn chips and watch television while you jog down here alone to secret private assignations. So they all ran, the couples, together but a bit apart, one of them always straining ahead to break free, to intercept another single broken-free jogger, with whom another brighter better faster bond could be made. The pelicans flew along the troughs between the waves, now you see them now you don't; the sandpipers ran across the wet sand, their tiny spindly wiry legs running left right left right left right too quick for the eye to discriminate, a blur of alternating motion. The track-suited ladies with their groomed dogs strode quickly through this stretch of beach, their skins taut from jazzercise all day and mud packs all night, did they use mud packs now?

'Nilus' slime,' said Lydia. 'It has amazing properties.'

He could believe it. He opened the car window. Breathed in. Deep. The salt spray of the sea. And was that a wisp of cannabis? Was that old kombi van there exhaling the herb on the evening breeze? And if not, why not?

'Hey, excuse me, you got a couple of bucks so I can get out of this town?'

A smiling face, young and much pitted, broken-nosed, tooth lost, came down level with them as they sat in their hire car upholstery, smiling in at Lydia.

'I need some bread for a ticket to get out of here.'

Marcus felt into his pockets, side pockets, top pocket.

The face came round by the back of the car and looked in on him, then suddenly clasped a hand across its eyes.

'Shit man, that jacket, it's kind of too much.'

The zig-zag English tweed vibrating.

'He's tripping,' said Lydia, 'ask him about dope if you want some.'

Marcus found a five dollar note in his top pocket, held it between first and second fingers.

'Ah, shit man, if I could I would man, they're so heavy man, I only just got out of jail, listen, look, I'll show you, look at this, read this, man.' He searched through his pockets and found a folded slip of paper. He opened it out and shook his head at it and flattened it smoother on the roof of the car. 'You'll see why I can't help.' He laughed. 'What a shit of a town,' he said.

It was a discharge slip from the county jail. Offence, possession of more than one ounce avoirdupois of a controlled substance.

'And my girlfriend, she's still in there. She hung around to come and visit me and we didn't have no money and then they put her in for shoplifting. So man, this is a town to get out of. They told me that. Get out of it, they said.'

Marcus handed him back the slip. And the five dollars.

'Thanks a lot, man. It all helps. Sorry I can't be of any assistance.' He gave them the peace sign. 'Shit man, that jacket, it kind of moves, you know, like it's strobing.'

'I know,' said Marcus.

He wandered off along the twilight beach edge, dissolved amidst the sand and spray and barking dogs and clouds of seagulls.

The sun set and they drove home.

'Getting closer, anyway,' said Marcus, trying to think positively, the Californian spirit, not to be a downer all the time, taking a bottle of Mexican beer from the supermarket sixpack in the fridge. He got very down when there was nothing to smoke.

'Oh, is that all?' said their landlady. 'I thought he was mad at me but I couldn't tell. I was going to ask you, was that being mad at me? I figured it was the washing machine. It sure makes a racket. Oh, you should've asked before. That's easy. How much do you want? I'll phone tonight.'

'Isn't that risky?'

'What's risky?'

'The phone?'

'Naaah, as long as it's under an ounce it's no problem. Just say how much you want and I'll give you a call.'

'Well, just under an ounce, tell her,' said Marcus, 'when she can get it.'

For Trees

The campus had its square brick buildings and its concrete tower blocks, not especially elegant, but solid and substantial and not cramped, there was that air of spaciousness, of a state where land stretched and buildings did not have to be piled close against each other. And some of the avenues had their trees, high imposing trees with ferns and spanish moss nestling in them, tucked in where a branch grew out of the trunk, delicate green fronds on winter-bare trees only now coming into leaf or blossom.

And then the teaching and administration buildings and the raw dormitory blocks surrendered to a human scale of low timber buildings, breakfast cafés, lunch bars, coffee shops, cluttered down in one corner of the campus, and I hung out here, eating eggs and hot cakes and maple syrup, drinking refills of coffee after coffee, lunching on baked burritos and draft beer, waiting till I gave my reading, watching the life of the students around, no obvious point of entry or connection available, an alien import flown in and soon to be flown out, listed in the campus paper, one of the endless stream of tokens and trophies and deals and exchanges and gambles and investments and loss leaders that passed this and every way, every day, every semester, every year: sitting watching, stretching out the coffee, stretching out the beer, so I didn't get too speedy, too drunk, too off the air for the audience that might or might not eventuate, living suspended in this capsule of otherness, flown in from somewhere no more rooted, no less alienated than this sense of suspension, wondering is this the life, advance purchase bargain discount stay over Saturday night required jet-setting, what grand design can this scratchy itinerary fulfil?

And at the other end of the campus the gaunt dormitory buildings surrender to tennis courts and other courts and pitches and then the wooden frame houses begin, modest, gentle, homely timber shelters with flowering trees around them and along the streets, I have caught it at this fine flowering moment of spring as all the trees break into bloom in the soft damp air. We detour to pick up some beer on the way, my host and I, and his wife pulls up behind us on a bicycle and walks along with us, gently campus town of flowering trees and bicycles and little timber houses warm in the soft afternoon air.

We sat round the potbellied stove while dinner cooked, sipping the local beer, talking of books and writers, when the tree feller came. We went out with him to look at the tree to be felled, not a big tree at all but one that if not felled right would crash through the roof, or worse, the neighbour's roof, a vigorous young tree in bud.

'We're building on out here,' said Jim. It was a tiny little house and they were stretching it back into the block, and the tree was growing where the house was to be. Maybe they could have stopped just short of it, maybe with a lot of difficulty they could have built right up to it, but that would no doubt have made it more difficult, a clear block was easier to work on, the roots would have been in the way of the foundations and if they'd left it probably the roots would have broken the foundations up. It was not my tree, not my house, not my business, this was logging country, thousands of trees were felled every day and sawn into timber for housing and pulped into paper for newsprint, books, notepads, where would I be without wood pulp, back to plague rags again?

'Shouldn't be any problem,' said the tree feller. 'Tomorrow morning.'

He took out his card and gave it to Jim. His partner's name had been scored through.

'Partnership dissolved?' Jim remarked.

'Oh, he got sick,' said the tree feller.

'An accident?' Visions of crashing timber, broken limbs, impaled organs.

'No, not exactly,' said the tree feller. 'He got mentally sick.'

'I'm sorry.'

'Yeah, well, he's in hospital now.'

'How's he getting along?'

'Oh, I don't think they'll be letting him out in a hurry,' said the tree feller. 'You might've read about it. It was in the papers. He got this belief the people next door were sperm banks for aliens. So he went in there and kind of hacked them to pieces. So—' He shrugged his shoulders. 'Anyway,' he said, 'tomorrow morning.'

At night I lay in the motel beside the river. The trees leaned over and whispered.

'He was right, you know,' they said. 'They were aliens. So are you, an alien. You are all aliens. But you can be open to us too. The spirits of the hamadryads can enter you and help us. Before the alien human came this was all forest. Everything you see was living timber. No Highway 99. No Best Western motel. No campus cleared for doubtful learning. This was the still soft land of the tree spirits and we lived here in peace. We hurt no-one. whoever heard of trees killing anyone till they started logging? Unless we were blown over in a gale and ourselves killed too, but that wasn't us, that was the windy elements.'

The newspaper lay on the wooden table. The wooden walls

kept out the wind. The spirits spoke through the dead timbers as if through a sounding box, like music through a flute or violin.

'Taking possession was not a good way,' they said. 'Taking possession never is. That is what we are trying to tell you. We do not want to chop up aliens. We do not want aliens to come and chop us up. It might have been a dramatic way of making our case. Timber terrorism. But we regret it. As we regret the daily felling of our fellow trees. So you can speak for us now. You can take our message. The airwaves would be preferable to paper and print. Readings. Even just speaking, talking. We have a case. We entrust it to you.'

The tree had been felled when I went back in the afternoon.

'You should've come round,' said Jim. 'It was beautiful watching a professional at work.'

We watched a bit of university baseball on television and then we cleared up the yard, Kathy and I passing timbers to Jim who sawed them with a power saw into lengths that would fit into the potbellied stove. Then we stacked the sawn lengths into a woodstack. It took us most of the afternoon, keeping us warm in the air that carried the sharp tinge of possible frost, our breath white plumes, our cheeks pink from the air and the exertion.

'This is about as much fun as anyone gets to have around here on a weekend,' Kathy said, as we looked at the completed woodstack.

Then we went in and had a few beers.

Music Making

'Hello,' he said. He was standing beside their table, just behind Marcus. They looked up in surprise because they didn't know anybody was there, yet the hello was said with such confidence. 'Hello, how are you?' Cicadas chattering in the soft evening, the tables out on the gravel beneath the vines. Then Lydia recognised him from the Rooms to Rent up the road, he'd called out to them as they went in from the beach, sitting outside one of the rooms set amidst the lemon grove. 'Kale spera,' they'd said. 'Francoises?' 'Oukhe, Australian.'

The rooms were out in the middle of nowhere, a couple of kilometres walk up from the beach. The restaurant was further along the road. From the tables they could see an inlet of the sea and the winking lights of the hydrofoil and along the shore blocks of houses and apartments. They'd thought they would have to walk to that town and finding the restaurant was a great relief.

'You're staying up there too,' Lydia said, pointing back to the Rooms to Rent, to be sure.

'Yes.'

'Where are you from?' she asked, continuing the earlier exchange.

'No,' he said, 'I'm working here, I'm a musician, we play at night here, sing, sometimes there's dancing.'

'Ah, that's you I hear at night,' Marcus said.

Every night, just after the family in the room next door had finished opening and shutting doors and shouting at their children and eating outside amongst the lemon trees and playing cards and listening to their radio and had settled down at last about midnight, there would be the amplified sound of music till two or three in the morning.

'Yes,' he said.

They were so tired and it was so hot, sweating sleepless in the little room, the mosquitoes purposefully targeting in through the windows, and the music going on and on.

It was good music, Lydia said, she didn't mind it. 'It's not someone's radio, it's live music.' Did that make it any easier to sleep through? It was so loud and he was so tired and it was so hot and he couldn't sleep. But Marcus didn't say this, not to the musician. He felt hypocritical not saying it since he'd said it so much in the hot, mosquito-ridden night, but he didn't.

'It's so hot,' the musician said. 'And I can't sleep. And every morning the woman in the next room wakes up at seven and goes yap yap yap.' He went yap, yap, yap with his hand, the fingers closing down on his thumb, yap yap yap. 'For two weeks now I have only four or five hours sleep a night. I am so tired. I am not playing well.' He took a packet of cigarettes out of his shirt pocket, fiddled around, delaying lighting one.

'You wouldn't be any better in our room,' said Lydia. 'The people next door just shout at each other all the time. We can't sleep either.' She didn't say anything about the music. It was Marcus who objected to the music, she liked music. 'You're here for the summer?'

'Yes, for the summer,' he said.

'Where do you work the rest of the year?'

'Athens.'

'As a musician?'

'Yes, of course. I play in a club there. But next year, maybe the year after, I open my own place. I am too old to play for other people all the time.'

We are all too old to play for other people all the time,

Marcus reflected. We do not have to be very old to be too old for that.

The insects cracked and exploded in the blue glow of the insect killing device. They would be glad when the music started so they didn't have to hear that.

'Excuse me,' he said, and gestured towards the restaurant building, taking out a cigarette and lighting it as he headed off there.

They watched the darkness fall over the still bay, one last water-skier towed across their line of vision, distant enough not to hear the noise of the motor boat.

'We should stay for the music,' Lydia said.

'We don't really need to.'

'It would be nice, though.'

'Except it's so late.'

'We might as well be here listening to it as not sleeping up there.'

The place was slowly filling up. It was clearly not the middle of nowhere for all these cars with French and Swiss plates, let alone for those with Greek ones.

He came by again and sat down. He refused a drink.

'I have to play soon,' he said. 'How long are you staying?'

'This is our last night. We have to get the early bus to get the ferry to go on south in the morning.'

'If I am up, I will take you to the ferry,' he said.

'No, no,' they said, 'that is very kind, but it is too early.'

'We will see,' he said. 'If I am awake . . .'

The grey wraith of sleepless nights wafted past.

'I have been to South America,' he said, 'and France and Spain. I have played there and collected songs. But never to Australia.'

'You should come,' Lydia said.

'Yes, but maybe for ten days, two weeks. Just to visit.'

'It's good.'

'Yes,' he said, 'but not to stay. Many people from here go there to stay. But I have my manager and my agent and Athens, I have always played in Athens.'

'And when you get your own club . . .'

'Of course,' he said. 'This year, maybe, next year, then . . .'

'Then you'll be busy.'

'I hope so,' he said. He stubbed out his cigarette. 'Excuse me, they are waiting now.'

Marcus hadn't even noticed the stage, a wooden sounding box with a back and sides and floor and roof. The other two musicians were there already, sitting down, plugging in their instruments, getting the microphones in position. They were ten years younger, in their late thirties. The one in the centre had a trimmed black beard and played a dulcimer, high piping notes cutting through the soft night. His eyes scanned the diners with a satisfied confidence, a sun king's delight at being on show, sitting up very straight, very erect, a cigarette held between his fingers even as he played. The other had an eager, out-reaching, smiling energy, playing guitar, nodding to people as they came in, and talking to the dulcimer player as they played. They had something going between them, musical, monetary, sexual, something that kept them interrelating and that excluded the older man. He had the flat white face and sad wiry mouth of a mime artist miming nothing but sadness, mouth tight and turned down at the corners, and none of the cocksure vibrancy of the others. After half a dozen songs he put down his guitar and left them in mid number, coming back with three glasses of wine. He put a glass within reach of each of the others, wordlessly, and then sat down again, took up his guitar, took a swig from his glass, and joined back in. There were no breaks between numbers, they played continuously, the bearded man in the centre singing and the other two doing backing vocals as they played, and then without any sign it had shifted and the older man was singing and the bearded man and his friend were backing. Now they were sad plaintive songs, Greek and French and Spanish ballads of sad cadences, and the diners came and left and talked and sometimes they sang along too. A little boy of about four came and stood out the front and clapped in rhythm, his eyes fixed wide on the musicians.

Neither Lydia nor Marcus knew any of the words. Just the mood of sad acceptance sang to them, plangent, the playing always sure and vigorous, and a world weariness the dominant theme. And their own weariness, of course. They had to leave to try and sleep to wake in time for the ferry. The music followed them up the hill and through the windows in the hot sweaty night. It was all peaceful back in the Rooms to Rent. The family next door were out, but they soon came back and shouted, drowning out the music for a while. But in the end even they went to bed and the music took over again and Lydia and Marcus lay they listening to it.

There was no sign of the musician outside his room the next morning. They got up early, Lydia and Marcus, and Marcus messed around to avoid waiting too long at the bus stop, and they missed the bus. They were tempted to take up the musician's offer and wake him, but they didn't, a cab went by, engaged, but the driver gestured that he would return, and he did, and they caught the ferry, and got to where they wanted to go, which was beautiful and quiet, though without any live music. But they had the music imprinted in their memories now, even if they didn't know the words and couldn't remember the tunes and never knew the man's name.

The Family

It was a heat wave again and the water of the harbour was evaporating and depositing a smell of stale piss everywhere. They could either have the windows shut and not sleep because it was so hot or have them open and not sleep because it was so noisy. The traffic went all night, and the sailors and the girls. Sailors in groups, Malaysian, Chinese, African, straggling in loose formation along the pavement and spilling into the road and looking at the strange bars and strange foods, circling round the nightclubs and strip joints. The names flashed in winking lights, ran the circuit of moulded neon tubes: Venus, Aphrodite, Circe.

Alex came to collect them. They hoped he would have a car but doubted that he would and he didn't.

'I did,' he said, 'gain my licence but I am not confident yet and the consequence was I had a small accident so I thought it would be better not to risk anything driving into the city.'

'Very wise,' said Lydia.

'So if that is all right with you we will take the train and then my father has arranged with a friend of his for when you return a taxi will arrive to take you back.'

Marcus had visions of astronomical taxi fares.

'We can get the train back,' he said.

'Oh yes, no problem. The taxi will take you to the station. My parents' house is some way from the station, not a long way, but the buses might not be running.'

Marcus would have liked just to have lain on the sheets of

the Hotel Daphne and drunk mineral water and maybe ventured out for coffee and baklava and come back safely into the cool. And now they had this epic journey ahead of them.

They walked to the station, past the nightclubs closed in the daytime, past the groups of bemused sailors, past the shops selling sandals and sunglasses and travelling bags, the sour smell of the harbour, the heat beating down on the pavements, stepping into the road to get past the stalls that had obtruded onto the pavements, and stepping back to avoid the cars and trucks, past the butchers' shops and the fish shops and the smell of dead flesh and the sight of severed limbs, gobbets of raw meat, still eyes.

'But if I practise as a lawyer,' said Alex, 'then I shall be serving the interests of corruption. It is made quite clear to me that that is the function of lawyers. But if I do not do that, then I have no function as a lawyer.'

The heat was truly phenomenal. They felt pummelled by it, it beat at them as if they were copper or bronze to be hammered into tables.

'They say over a thousand people have died,' said Alex. 'It is rumoured that the authorities are unable to cope with the situation. The mortuaries are crowded to overflowing. They have had to commandeer public buildings to contain the bodies.'

It did not provide the usual joy, this further evidence of authority failing to cope. Not with a vision of school-rooms stuffed with cadavers.

And it wasn't that hot. It was hot but surely not that hot.

'They do not have the facilities to cope with the situation. When a real disaster strikes, they are impotent,' said Alex.

'It's the same everywhere,' said Lydia.

'But they don't admit their inability until it is too late,' said Alex.

'It's already too late,' said Marcus.

'I think perhaps it is,' said Alex. 'Since Chernobyl the food has been contaminated. We were told to stay indoors. Crops had to be destroyed, but one suspects much of it was not destroyed but sold. As for AIDS, I have heard on good authority that it is widespread here too. The authorities announce that after swimming here now you should shower. The beaches are so crowded, there are so many people now swimming in the sea with disease.'

Now he tells us, Marcus groaned. Inwardly, but no less a groan. After these weeks of swimming and eating, now we find out everything is contaminated, the world is doomed.

In the end the station was there, the great high building, the scuffle over payment, Alex insisting that he provide their tickets, and then the wait. They stood there, out of the sun, but the heat pressed all around them, as trains came and waited and went out again. They looked for the sign of their destination but it was never there, as Alex told them about listening to the BBC World Service to improve his English.

'I have the program guide,' he said. 'I find it most useful.'

Marcus looked through it, calming his desperation.

'I think,' said Alex, 'I think perhaps something is wrong. I will go and inquire.'

He came back. They were on the wrong platform. This was the platform the train used to depart from, now it had been changed.

They walked round to the correct platform and a train arrived within a few minutes and soon they were off, through the suburbs, and then underground, from one end of the city to the other, why are we doing this, in a heat wave, this is ridiculous, this is hell, this is insufferable, past the point of no return, the recognised stops in the centre of the city, couldn't they just escape here, up to the blinding sun of the pavements, find a pavement café, drink something cool, recover, return to the hotel, and sleep the day out till twilight, and on they rattled in the crowded carriage, the train stopped, everybody out, out onto the platform to wait for another train, this one arbitrarily having decided despite its displayed destination to go no further, that's how I feel, thought Marcus, but how can I resist, refuse, why are we doing this, onto the next train and out to the country.

Then they got a drink at the station and felt better, ready to do battle with the taxis that swept past and the buses that didn't come or had just gone, Alex tentatively suggesting possibilities, the sun still beating down, remorselessly hot and no reason to hope for relief, you had to be quick to grab a taxi, in the end Lydia flagged one down, it stopped for her, and they all piled in.

But out at the house it was worth it.

'Pull your chair out,' said Alex's mother, on the edge of the verandah the breeze swept past, 'pull your chair into the breeze,' which filtered through the pear trees and the high straggly eucalypts and cooled them as they sat there, coffee, baklava, pears, the garden green and vibrant around them, the country quiet, calm.

'Not for me,' said Alex, refusing baklava, crème caramel. The grandmother insisted, then the mother, refusing his refusals. He tapped his teeth, a desperate strategy. They rejected it. Since when had he so suddenly developed a toothache?

'Now,' he said, 'now I have heard everything, first I am too thin, then I am too weak, not I am a liar. This family, it is impossible, how much longer can I tolerate it?'

His face was anguished, that true anguish of impossible desperation, of the insolubility of the family situation.

'Now she says I am making a scene and being impolite,' he translated. 'Yet it is never I who makes the scene. I simply decline to eat baklava and crème caramel. This is an insult.

This is unacceptable. But they cannot accept that I cannot eat baklava and crème caramel. Not even on a hot day after a long train journey. Always it is like this, day after day.' 'They care for you,' said Lydia. 'It is just a mother's way of showing she cares.'

'Stuffing me up like I am a goat for the market,' said Alex.

'Just families,' said Marcus. 'It's always the same.'

'I think not,' said Alex.

'In different ways,' said Marcus. 'Different manifestations, same effect.'

'I do not think I can continue to live here,' said Alex.

'I went twelve thousand miles away,' said Marcus. 'And when I come back, even now, it is still the same.'

Was that why he had gone twelve thousand miles away? Was that the reason? Had there been a reason or had it just happened, just for a job, unthought, unplanned?

When the afternoon heat had begun to drop Alex said he would take them for a walk. They went out through the garden with its rows of tomato plants, its pear trees, its fig trees, and took a dusty track past other houses with their closed gardens, out to more open land. In the distance they could see the beginnings of the suburbs. But here they were still at the edge of the country, houses for escape from the city heat, smallholdings.

'I have a friend who has a small farm, would you like to visit it? He keeps chickens.'

There were long low sheds beneath high trees. The land itself was untended, brown grass, dusty tracks. The farm was in the long sheds, row upon row of hens in their permanent boxes, factory egg production, batteries which they never left.

It was too horrible. This was the reality beyond the imagination. The way we treat poultry now. Alex went into the sheds looking for his friend. Marcus walked away, avoiding encountering Lydia's reactions, there was nothing that could be said that would change any of it, insist on free-range eggs, he shut his ears to the sound of the hens, turned his back so he did not look inside the shed doors.

They walked down the track to the house and the friend's mother asked them in. She was in black, that habitual black, but this was a recent widowhood and her sadness pervaded them as they sat on the verandah. Alex translated her grief for them as Lydia said words of consolation insofar as consolation could be said which Alex translated and the widow and Lydia held hands and held back tears. They sat there awhile, shaded by high straggling gum trees and dark cypresses, drinking lemonade from fresh lemons. Alex's friend drove up but it was the day to deliver eggs to the shops, this was the busy day, so they left him loading up his car and walked back.

They passed the stables where rich city-dwellers kept their horses.

'The girls who work here all come from England,' Alex said. 'From Surrey. I tried to talk to them, since I am always glad of an opportunity to practise my English. But they seemed as if they did not want to talk to me.'

'I find the same thing with girls from Surrey who ride horses,' said Marcus. 'I wouldn't take it personally.'

'But I am worried about it nonetheless,' said Alex. 'I wondered if I had perhaps said something wrong. I would have liked to talk about England and English society and politics but they would say nothing.'

'It's just the way they are,' said Marcus. 'They probably don't have anything to say.'

'They also eat very badly. I looked in the room of one of them. There were all these chocolate bar wrappers and empty coca-cola cans. I think that is all they lived on. It is very unhealthy.'

'They probably can't cook.'

'Is that possible?'

'They were probably brought up with everything done for them and don't know how to'—he would have said boil an egg, but did not want to bring that scene of the batteries up again—'how to do anything.'

'At this house,' Alex said, 'there was a terrible tragedy. There was a daughter who was very protected. She was not allowed to go out alone or to have boyfriends. The parents were very strict, very traditional. And then it turned out that one of her father's friends was seeing her and had this relationship. And when the father confronted his friend to denounce him, he got in a rage, the father, and collapsed with a heart attack and died. There are so many stories like this.'

Dusty lanes, unobtrusive houses, electric power lines strung on poles, high wire fences, vines, sunflowers, dark cypresses.

Back at the house the father was home, waiting for them to join him in an ouzo, sitting out in the garden, chairs by the little shed where he kept his wine.

'This is his ritual, every evening,' said Alex. 'I am afraid that we do not get along.'

'Fathers and sons, it is always like this,' said Lydia.

'Not always, I think,' said Alex. 'There are people I know who can co-exist amicably. But not here.'

He was short, stocky, the father, whereas Alex was thin, tall. The father came out from his shed bearing the ouzo bottle, poured Lydia and Marcus a drink in the small, sturdy glasses whose very shape and texture asserted the strength of the drink they had to withstand. Alex refused. But they needed him there, Alex, to translate.

'Very good,' said Marcus, 'tell your father, excellent.'

Alex muttered the compliment. Marcus's glass was immediately refilled.

'No, no,' he said, 'no more.'

'It will do no good,' said Alex, 'whatever you say.'

They complimented him on the garden, the father.

'Hard work,' Alex translated for them. 'It is just by hard work, he says.'

'I can see,' said Marcus.

'But the implication is that he alone does the hard work. The implication is that I am just a parasite,' said Alex.

'Tell him,' said Lydia, 'how good your English is. Tell him that we are very impressed with your command of English. You do an excellent job of translating.'

Alex demurred, finally did as he was told, and the father replied to them.

'He says, but what is the use? He asks, will that feed us all? He says it should be excellent after all these years of studying. But when will it be useful and I will get a job?'

The father grinned at them, severely, but there was a grin in it, a smile of pride.

'When the time comes,' said Lydia, 'you will get an excellent job. Tell him that.'

Alex hesitated, but told him.

The father threw up his hands.

'He does not believe, you see. He does not believe that these years of study are of any use. And now that I do not intend to practise law, he cannot understand what good that studying was. He would like me to go out and get a job tomorrow.'

The cicadas punctuated the evening with their drilling, one, two, setting the note and then the whole cooperative chorus, the whole garden vibrating. The father went round checking on his plants, the evening's last patrol, before they were called for dinner.

They ate on the verandah, a huge, splendid meal.

'My father asks, what will you drink?' Alex said.

'Not a lot,' said Marcus.

'There is no escape, you must drink something. Always I refuse and always I have to.'

'Ah, well,' said Marcus, 'what does everybody else drink?'

'There is beer or there is wine. I shall drink beer as I do not enjoy the wine.'

'And what does your father drink?'

'Ah, my father drinks wine. It is his own wine, he is very proud of it, he would be very happy if you would drink his wine. Myself, I do not enjoy it.'

Marcus drank wine and made the father and himself very happy. Between them they demolished one bottle, then another, the evening glowed into a vibrant golden resinous fragrance. The soft air, the air carrying the soft smell of the fig trees, the delicate ripening pears, and the meal with its seemingly endless succession of items whose identity dissolved in the glorious glow of the retsina, the cheers and good healths, the clinking of glasses held against each other in toasts of goodwill.

'My father insists I translate to you again. Now he is getting drunk and I have already translated this several times.'

'That's all right,' said Marcus.

'He wishes your excellent health and success and says you must come and visit again. He says you remind him of an Englishman he knew in the war, they had many good evenings drinking together. There, that is the last time I will translate that. Now he is drunk and he forgets he repeats himself.'

'That's the nature of getting drunk,' said Marcus. 'Tell him how excellent his wine is and how marvellous his hospitality. Or did I already say that?'

Alex told him, anyway.

'Oh no,' he said, 'I cannot bear it. He asks me to repeat to you exactly what I have already repeated only two minutes ago.'

'It's very hard translating for people getting drunk,' said Lydia. 'You're doing an excellent job.'

'Sometimes I find it unbearable,' said Alex. 'I feel I am not the son they wanted, I am not strong, I do not drink wine, I do not have a job, I refuse to compromise and become a practising lawyer, sometimes I feel absolutely desperate.'

His eyes flashed black fire.

'It's just families,' said Marcus.

'It will get better,' said Lydia.

'No it won't,' said Marcus. 'It's always the same and it's always terrible. That's the way they generally are. Some people are lucky and for them it's all happy. But for most of us it's conflict and difficulty and resentment.'

'I think you might be right but I wish that you were not,' said Alex.

'I think so too, and I wish the same,' said Marcus.

Lydia disagreed. 'It will get better.'

'Cheers,' said the father, raising his glass. Marcus raised his and they clinked them together above the table.

'Cheers.'

Maison de la Vie

'I've been to the Maison de Balzac and I've been to the Maison de Victor Hugo.'

'Ah,' he said, 'but you must go to the Maison de la Vie. It costs ten francs to enter the Maison de Balzac, ten francs to enter the Maison de Victor Hugo, but the Maison de la Vie—'

'Is free?' I said.

'No, no. Nothing is free. But with the Maison de la Vie you have already paid the entrance fee. Now all that is required is the supplement.'

'How much is the supplement?' I asked.

He laughed. 'If I could tell you that I could tell you everything,' he said. 'It depends on the hours you travel. It depends on the speed or convenience with which you wish to go. If you want to pass through with minimum inconvenience, then it will be different from stopping at every station.'

'What, more?'

'Perhaps,' he said. 'Perhaps not. It depends. More for which? Which way do you want to travel?'

'Well,' I said, 'it depends.'

'On the price?' he said. 'You would determine the course of your life according to the price of the supplement? You are some sort of rich boy? Or a clochard, maybe. Maybe you would rather sleep on the grilles of the metro. Then it will only cost you one ticket. Four francs maybe, less than five francs. That way you can keep warm at night.'

'And alternatively?'

'Alternatively? For some there is no alternative. For some it is better neither to travel nor arrive, for some it is better to sleep on the grilles of the metro than walk the banks of the Seine and gaze at the cold waters. You've seen them. Surely even you on your way to the museums have seen them, leaning on the parapets, walking slowly and indeterminately because, after all, there is nowhere they are going except to the terminus. Which the Seine offers but it is a cold way to go. So they look at it. Meditatively, you suggest. Singing strange songs, you imagine, singing familiar songs, would that be preferable? While the current sweeps past. There is no further entrance fee for that. But the exit charges: to die without insurance, that is something else again.'

'Exit charges?'

'But of course. You throw away your ticket, how are you going to get out? The Maison de la Vie lies all about you and you are trapped in the tunnels beneath. Or swept past on the current and you see, on the embankment there, everything you ever desired: second-hand books, girls, postcards and pavement cafés.'

'Is that all I ever desired?'

'Maybe just the postcards now,' he said. 'Mementoes of where you might have been. You can scribble on the back and who is ever to know whether you were there or not, whether you intended to go but failed to find the time, or maybe saw from the distance the tower, the windmill, the national costume. Or maybe it was one of those second-hand cards, those pre-owned antiquities of a prelived life. And an inscription in faded ink. "We met here beneath the pyramids aeons ago." And who will ever know whether you did or will, whether the pyramids were ever there, or will be. And without the price of the postage you will carry the card around, from Maison to Maison, increasingly crumpled in your pocket, between the passport and the shredded tissues, the address a fading will, the insignia of kisses and dying

137

hope, the address smudging, running, like mascara dissolving in tears. "Is this," you will ask, "a life?" Souvenirs of Victor Hugo holding his head, always his hand on his head, fixed in eternal sadness; or Balzac in his capuchin's robe, eternally ready to write, but the writing table immobilised in the Maison, not to be touched, highly polished and free of ink, free of paper. You will sneak a touch when the attendant is in another room. The tears will flood up into your fingers through your arms and gather in the corners of your eyes: for the unwritten novels, for the unlived life, who can tell you? The attendant returns and you are asked not to touch. You sniff back the tears. They remain unshed. In the Maison de Victor Hugo the quills are beneath glass. The ink, if it had been there, would have turned to powder. Buy your cards, buy your posters, buy your umbrella in the boulevard to shelter you from the tears of the sky. It is dry in these Maisons, but even you will have to walk along the streaming streets when you leave.'

Armistice

So I go to see my aunt to say goodbye again, she is ninety and this could be the last goodbye, my mother has been saying this for twenty years now, it might be the last time you see her, and it never is, but one time it will be, and she tells me the same stories again that I never listen to, having heard them so many times with deaf ears, refusing to listen to their insistent message.

'What have you been doing?' she asks, perfunctorily.

'Picking apples,' I say.

'Has your mother got someone to pick the rest of them?'

Always failure, always incompletion, a good job never well done.

'I've got them all,' I say. 'The ones the ladder will reach. It needs a longer ladder than we have to get the rest.'

'Oh, those young sailors,' she says, 'I'm always terrified when they climb up, I'm always afraid they might slip, they've been trained but they're so young. Four of them climb up in time to the music, those huge high masts, and then the one climbs to the top and they drop the petals. There's a petal for every one of the dead in the two great wars, millions of petals.

'There would be,' I said.

'I've been remembering my war service,' she said, 'the risks I took.'

In the old peoples' home the heat pumps through the radiators like Zyklon-B. Dad would never visit there, he couldn't breathe in the heat. I used to think it was just an excuse, a rationalisation for his choice of economy and cold, a resentment against the squander of tax-payers' money. Sure he was dying of emphysema from the years as a moulder. There were good reasons not to visit. Now I sit there and swelter.

'This soldier was back from the front,' she said. 'He said, you've been here too long, you should go to the war office. He wrote such a well written letter. It was so good I couldn't send it. I only copied out part of it. Such a nice boy. A public school boy.'

No doubt.

'I volunteered,' she said. 'They only took volunteers. It was a huge big building. And inside were walls, and then more walls, and there were two of you at a time in these little forts. You were locked in your own little fort, just two at a time packing the powder. Then if there was an explosion only the two of you were killed in your own little fort. You were only there for half an hour at a time. If you breathed in the powder for too long at a time you got sick. One time there was a huge explosion. We never knew how many were killed. It was all military secrets. I wasn't there when it happened. Some of the powder had got on my stomach and made me sick and I was off for a few days at home. In the end I had to transfer. The powder was getting on my stomach and making me sick. That was when I went to the war office. I was one of the last five to leave the war office. Those were marvellous times. But I was so frightened cycling home at night. We had to work late and I had to cycle two or three miles from the station, along a country road, and my friend went one side of the Park and I had to go the other, down through a paddock, up and down this bumpy road, I went smack into a cow one night, and then into the barn, and there were no lights, and I had to leave my bicycle in the barn and walk through to the other end and out into the yard. Mother was never game to come and look for me. Someone asked her once wasn't she worried about her daughter having to cycle home alone late through the dark. "I've got four little ones to look after," she said, "I'm so busy getting them all off to bed I don't have time to worry about anything else." I remember this officer on the station one night. "Aren't you afraid to be alone on the station at this time of night?" he said. "Well, it's war work and I volunteered and it has to be done," I said. He was a young public school boy. He was off to the front. There were all sorts of people in the war office, well educated people, clergymen's daughters and doctors' daughters and solicitors' wives. I did enjoy those times. Do you remember the Banks, they were county people, Mr Banks said something about a battalion and I said, "That's a thousand men." "How did you know that?" he said. "I used to work in military records," I said, he was impressed.

All those years of refusing to join the school cadet corps, marching for CND, anthologising against the Vietnam War, are they all in vain? Has she never registered them, is she now in a world of her own like she always was, or is this to shame me for not wearing a poppy for Armistice Day, for not being patriotic, for being an expatriate, for not having gone to public school, for her sister's having married an iron moulder, a job not only proletarian but a reserve occupation. She shows me the long roll of photograph of the war office, seventy years ago, officers, boots, moustaches, hierarchies.

Ah, dear aunt, you taught me about the sub-text, you showed me how narration transmitted ideology, sometimes I even think you helped drive me into exile, you and the world to which you subscribe, the dominant world, the world whose ideas are the dominant ideas, whose art is the dominant art in every age. You proclaimed those values to me, Sunday after Sunday when you came round to tea, and at every opportunity in between. It is only right I should record something of them, those values that thrust me unavoidably if not unambiguously into the ranks of resistance, of refusal, for that alone you deserve our gratitude. The future may be ours but we can afford a moment to remember how the present still belongs to you.

Watching the
Ferry Come In

At first we thought he was a police agent. Sitting outside the café, his coffee, his glass of water stretched out through the afternoon. Our suspicions illuminating more about us than him. But he was noticeable in the ways others were not. He was not a taxi driver, he had no cab waiting beside the tables. He was not a café owner. He wore nondescript grey trousers, fading blue work shirt. But he was not speckled with plaster or paint from restoring a house. Nor did he have a basket of jars of honey-roasted almonds, or bouquets of dried flowers to sell. He was regularly there, yet not quite of it, sometimes talking to the café owner or some of the men, but as often as not just sitting there alone. No doubt that was how we noticed him, also regularly there, and even less part of it. And sometimes reading or making notes on one of the rickety raffia chairs at a wobbling wooden table beneath the shading trees. The old men sat there with their coffees or their beers but they did not read. By the time the newspapers reached the island another day had passed, there were other lies, other columns of misinformation, if you were interested you could listen to the radio. If they sat there arguing about politics it was not on the basis of newspaper reports. They sat there placidly, when they sat there. And more often than not worked their patch of land and didn't sit there. The Sunday market, yes, they would come in for that. But he was there all through the week.

Yet to deduce from this he did not work his plot of land would have been wrong. It was his land that kept him. Giorgios the taxi driver told us. He was explaining why the taxi could not be hired some day one week. Giorgios had been a ship's engineer, now he drove a taxi and was working on his house. His crazy house, he called it. Even worse than the house was the garden. He had arranged for Petros to help him prepare his tomato patch. Petros the philosopher. For years he had studied at Heidelberg. The heavy black-framed glasses. They were what was different. Not the cord round his waist for a belt. Not the shoes dusty from walking down to the harbour from the hills on the hot unsurfaced road. But the heavy glasses. The black frames to the eyes. The dark reflections on existence. The philosopher.

Giorgios laughed. 'They found some inscriptions,' he said, 'they were excavating on the mainland. They sent messages for him to come and decipher them. "No," he said, "no, I am too busy, my tomatoes are nearly ripe, I have to tend them."'

And when he wasn't tending his tomatoes, on the days the ferry called from the mainland he would walk down the hot dusty road to the harbour and sit at the café by the jetty and drink a coffee and read his book and watch the activity, of people coming and going from the ferry, the trucks, the cars, the marks of change, the despair of departures, the hopes of arrivals, the recurrent flux.

'What would you do if you gave up this job?' Chris asked, not long before he did.

'Go away,' I said, 'go away and live on an island.'

'But what would you do with yourself?'

'Try and grow tomatoes, I suppose,' I said.

'And when you got bored?'

'You could always go down and watch the ferry come in.'

The Beauties
of Sydney

The idea was to go sailing.

'I will take you sailing,' said Rolof, 'I will show your English poet some of the beauties of Sydney.'

The water, the bush, the sun, the light.

'We will have a picnic,' said Rolof, 'we will sail out and have lunch and look at the beauties of Sydney. Bring some food. Bring some wine.'

We got all that arranged, the food, the wine.

'Bring warm clothes in case there is a wind.'

We did that too.

'Can we take a train?' asked Jon.

We told him there was no train we could take.

'Are you sure?'

'Yes.'

He looked disbelieving. Britain's imperial glories, the age of steam. Or was it ecologically sound mass transit systems?

'I'm sure there's a train,' he said. 'I can sense it.'

'He's becoming psychic as the years pass,' said Lorna. 'It's a ghost train. It's your impending mortality, Jon.'

He stood there, sniffing the air.

'Maybe it's the old tramline,' we conceded, 'but it was ripped out years ago.'

'No, it's a train,' he insisted.

'He believes if he sniffs hard enough it will materialise,' said Lorna.

'Maybe it's the light rail line they've been talking about for years.'

'Yes,' said Jon.

'But they haven't built it yet.'

'Are you sure?' he said.

We bundled him into the car, his eyes fixed on the future. We drove up the coast and parked at the wharf and took the ferry to the island.

'Welcome,' said Rolof, 'you have escaped civilisation. Now you can begin to live. Or die. As the case may be.'

We had expected to go to his house, open a beer, have a coffee, extend the endless deferral of the hazards of nature, maybe a tempest would blow up and we could just sit peacefully indoors. But no. Rolof was there at the wharf and the dinghy was waiting.

'Guests first,' said Rolof.

Jon looked at it apprehensively.

'Are we sailing in this?'

'This is to take us to the boat,' Rolof said. He gestured across to the expanse of Pittwater. Somewhere out there was the chosen vessel.

'Can't you bring it to the wharf?' Jon asked.

'Only if I run aground and crack the hull,' said Rolof. 'The tide is out. I have to moor in deep water.'

'Couldn't we wait till the tide comes in?' asked Jon.

'You want to wait all day?' said Rolof. 'Here? You want to eat your picnic on the cargo wharf while we could be looking at the beauties of Sydney? When the tide comes in it will be too dark to see any of the beauties. The dusky maidens will be lost in the dusk.'

The mermaids danced in the gentle waves, beckoning. The sirens sang their seductive songs, alluring. Rolof was impatient to be strapped to the mast and block the ears of his guests with wax.

'I take your point,' said Jon.

'That's something,' said Lorna.

It was a very little dinghy, it was indeed. But it took four, Rolof and Jon and Lorna and my girlfriend. And the loaves and the wine and the cheese and the olives and the tomatoes and the cucumbers; everyone bulky in their sweaters and jackets, this was a winter expedition. I waited on the wharf with Rolof's wife and Bobbie, the publisher. Visitors first. The last deferral.

We watched them sink. It was nothing immediately dramatic. They seemed very low in the water and as Rolof rowed to the yacht they got steadily lower. Perhaps the oars shipped water. Perhaps there was a wash from a passing power boat. Perhaps there was a wave. Perhaps there was a crack in the hull.

The certainty was they were sinking. Slowly. But none the less inevitably for that. We watched dumbstruck as they sunk lower, the water up to the very gunwales. What could we say, could we believe the evidence of our eyes?

Rolof spoke for us.

'We are sinking,' he called out, in surprised yet authoritative tones, the captain of his craft. 'Prepare for the water, we are about to sink.'

We waited to see them slowly immerse.

But Jon had heard somewhere that when a ship sank it created a vortex that sucked you down with it. He decided to leap clear. The dinghy dipped and capsized and they were all in the water. The loaves floated away. The wine sank without trace.

'Help!' called Jon, flapping his tweed-jacketed arms, 'help, help, I can't swim.'

'He can't swim!' exclaimed Rolof, spluttering as he rose and spluttering as he heard, 'His book is called *The Principle of Water* and he can't swim! What principle is that? That is the principle of drowning.'

Mortification transmuted to the satisfactions of irony, he was saved from having to go down with his ship, now he need only choke in joke. His own book was called *From Another Shore.* He headed for it.

'Hey,' said Bobbie, always the publisher, 'this is great. Author of *Principle of Water* Drowns. This'll be great publicity, this'll get the feature pages, we'll sell some books with this.'

'Help,' called Jon, surfacing again, 'help.'

There was a lifebelt, one of those traditional, white circular ones, hanging at the wharf. I went to get it. But already paradox, the title of Rolof's next book, had unnerved me. These were the lifebelts you threw at drowning people and hit them on the head and knocked them unconscious so they could never reach out or hold on. I threw it cautiously and missed Jon by yards that he could not swim.

There was a barge moored to the wharf. Somebody standing there started its motor so we could head out and pick them all up. But we forgot to untie one of the mooring ropes and the barge jerked to a halt and tightened the knot immovably.

'Help!' Jon called, surfacing for the third time.

The women rescued him. They supported him between them and towed him ashore.

'How can a poet not swim?' asked Rolof, salvaging his captain's honour and the oars and the upturned dinghy.

The women scrambled ashore and dragged Jon up with them. They took off their waterlogged tweed jackets and wrung them out above the tide line, beside the bushes, next to the shell midden. Rolof restored the lifebelt to its post.

The barge motor was shut down. In the silence we could hear the kookaburras laughing.

'Nothing lost,' said Rolof, 'only the bread of life. I will dive for the wine tomorrow. Now we will walk up to the house and get dry and I lend you some clothes and then we can go. There is still time.'

'No,' said Jon, 'no, I don't think so.'

'What, you are not afraid, just a little dip, we get dry and you will see.'

'No,' said Jon.

Bobbie had already headed up to the house to phone the press.

Lorna put her jacket back on. Suddenly she screamed.

'A spider, a great black spider!'

'They're deadly poisonous if it was a funnel web,' said Rolof's wife. 'The island's full of them.'

'Hysteria,' said Rolof, 'delayed shock, it's nothing,' brushing it away, whatever wasn't there. 'We will walk up to the house and have a shower and get dry and then we shall all be calm and then we go for our sail.'

'No, no, no, no, no,' Jon howled like a ghost train in the eternal night.

Lorna stood shaking on the rocks, shaking her jacket, shaking with horror.

'You'll see,' said Rolof, 'you'll be safer on the water, no spiders there. Nothing but the beauties of Sydney.'

I Like Him to Write

S uddenly there were all these biographers working on her life. After the years of neglect, after the twenty years in which she could get nothing new published, after she was dead. She would have been appalled. She had burned all her manuscripts and most of her papers. But other people had letters, letters she had written to them. Some of them were already in library collections, letters to other writers she had known who had sold, or whose executors had sold, their papers. And now they were being tracked down. When he was in the States at that pointless symposium he was told by some silvered scoundrel that his name turned up in her correspondence.

'Oh yes,' he said. It was breakfast in the seedy, expensive hotel they had been booked into. He'd joined the silvered scoundrel on the principle that people who leave you out of bibliographies they've compiled may as well be wooed, nothing is gained by boycotting them, they've already boycotted you, but if you manage a veneer of civility they might restore you in a second edition. They might. Nothing much is lost, anyway, the alternative is eating your pancakes in sickly, syrupy silence.

'She speaks generously of you.'

'Oh, that's nice,' he said. 'I knew her for a while towards the end of her life.'

They were up on the fifteenth floor but the view wasn't anything special. Still, you could get as much coffee as you liked for no extra charge. The scoundrel went off and brought more.

'Where is her correspondence?' he asked.

'Oh, scattered, I imagine. This was in the —— collection. He was an old friend of hers.'

'So there are letters from her to him?'

'Quite a lot.'

He should have asked why the scoundrel was going through the —— collection, but he didn't. He didn't know anything about —— who was no-one he'd ever read, later he found out —— had worked on one of the left reviews of the thirties. Not the sort of writer you'd expect the silvered scoundrel to be studying.

'Are you still at wherever it was?' he asked him.

It appeared he wasn't. Now he was on secondment, some sort of research fellow, writing reports on the archives, nosing through the new purchases of old correspondence.

He felt tacky as if the maple syrup had crawled all over him.

But he was glad she had said nice things about him. He'd felt bad about losing contact with her, he felt bad about still not having written the things about her work that he knew he must, now he felt good that he was in the literary archives. Even if he was left out of the bibliographies.

He had written asking her to contribute to a volume by writers opposing the American and Australian and other allies' war in Vietnam. She responded promptly and wrote a piece especially for the collection, which he hadn't expected. Most people simply sent something they had already written. She wrote again a week or so later apologising for the messy typescript. She had been hurrying to get it into the post and she hadn't been well that day so didn't feel up to typing it again. Later she found out she'd had a mild heart attack.

He was appalled. Moved that she should have worked on the piece in that state, touched at her commitment, appalled that some peremptory deadline of his might nearly have killed her. How mild was a mild heart attack?

He didn't know much about her. At that time she was pretty much lost from view. He had read some of her books but they weren't the sort of thing he was writing himself at that point. At that point he was caught up with the 'new' and had yet to see the reactionary consequences of that aesthetic of the new, the focus on form, on manner, the agenda of exclusions. In the end he saw it, in the end he came to understand the way she had written. But by then it was too late, by then she was dead. No, it wasn't too late, the books were there, there to learn from, there to take heart from. The point about writers is you learn from their writing. Meetings are peripheral. It is their writing that teaches, the example of their writing that holds out the torch. This first encounter, this encounter by writing, would always be there as a lesson for him. The lesson of commitment.

'I trust I did not pass as any American agent,' she wrote to him in one of their first exchanges of letters. She was explaining why she had said 'somewhere (in one of my several asinine speeches) that the Australians should not look quite so much to their past; but think of other countries, too, and I mentioned the USA, comparable if very different. I trust I did not pass as any American agent for that remark. But with the Americans having so much influence now in Australia and using our men for their wars, it would not be a bad idea for Australians to know something about this great, fierce, turbulent, gifted and dangerous country . . .'

But it was always the other way round. Here he was, here they all were, in America, at a symposium on Australia, delivering their best thoughts, their latest analyses, eagerly informing on their own nation, handing over everything and learning what? Initially he'd refused. 'I've spent my travel funds,' he said, he had. 'Oh, that's no problem, we can cover that.' 'You should go,' said one of his scoundrel colleagues, 'if you've got your eye on the chair it's important you go to something like this.' He went. He didn't get the chair.

At the hotel a display board listed the conferences in residence. Reunion of women FBI officers. He had dinner with another of his scoundrel colleagues who had been visiting Washington, or outside Washington, Langley Virginia no doubt. There'd been lots of dope there. 'You still smoke, don't you? Do you grow it? I should have brought you some.'

'Yes, you should've,' he agreed. He ordered himself another beer and a mineral water for the colleague.

'What was it they had against you in the department?'

'Against me?'

'That confrontation you had?'

'Confrontation?'

'Yes, what was the issue?'

'I didn't know there was one,' he said. Or did this little prick know something? Or was he just fishing?

Another night there was an ex-student who sought him out. They had a drink too. An escape from colleagues.

'This place is terrible, let's go to a bar,' said the ex-student who was over there on a fellowship and knew the bars and dives.

They set off into town, he and the ex-student and a literary theorist who specialised in suspicion. The ex-student chattered amiably leading them down mean streets. It was like those movie scenes where the set becomes deserted, a sinister silence reigns, and someone has been lured to destruction.

'Just a moment,' said the theorist, 'where are we going?'

'Not much further,' said the ex-student.

'No,' said the theorist of suspicion, 'no, I don't like this, I'm not going any further.'

Once he would have laughed, gone on with the ex-student. But this time he was relieved at the theorist's intransigence. The ex-student laughed alone. They went back to the terrible hotel.

There were dinners, buffets, receptions, where the visitors met the faculty and the graduate students. It was what they called a distinguished faculty, but not many of them showed up. It was all a bit marginal to the interests of the great names, this Australian literature, even if you put it in the post-colonial literature category, new literature, world literature written in English. But there were graduate students on fellowships there, privileged young persons from the developing third world preparing to go back and rip off their peasantry and new proletariat. He was getting drunk and sentimental and outraged and no-one there with whom to share his dreams of a better life.

He had sent her his first novel. She wrote back: 'I was looking for something relaxing to read and I enjoyed it very much. It rested me for some reason and I had three nights of good dreams—not sexy, by the way; (I expect you work it all out in your book); but to cause good dreams I think is a compliment to an author. Well, not sexy—the first night I dreamed of the good Dr (interested in Vietnam, you know him); the second such an odd dream about my late—we were taking a long walk along the Gap cliffs at Watson's Bay and some workmen in bell tents had planted geraniums in the crumbling kerosene shale—I greatly admired the workmen for this! The third night I dreamed about Stalin! (But he was a very attractive loafing Romeo.) Well, I am glad, for I am not dreaming much at the moment, leading such a dull (kind, good) life.'

One of the swarm of people announcing they were writing books on her gave a paper at the symposium. He was glad she was now a subject for discussion after having been for so long obliterated from the literary record. And now the left was being washed away again, more subtly this time, there were none of the martyr-making public inquisitions, just silent suppressions, and wave after wave of new literary theories whose one coherence was the displacement of a discourse of the left. And here they were at the beach-head of literary theory, where the raw materials were shipped in cheaply from Europe and the manufactured product assembled and distributed throughout the world. In this context, where it was pretty well all evasion and rubbish, the paper didn't seem any worse than anything else, and its theoretical naivety no bad thing. It offered a psychological profile, her books noticed only insofar as they filled out the casebook. At least it meant that she was mentioned, and even at this point he still believed that just to be there was something, better to be present and dealt with clumsily than to be elided altogether. So someone who at least dealt with her couldn't be all bad, could they? Well, that of course was a mark of his particular theoretical naivety. And that, allied with his automatic sympathy for underdogs, led him into deep error. Since the sophisticates had consigned the paper to the rubbish bin, what could he do but speak to its author and say how he'd enjoyed it, standing in the hotel lobby beneath the proclamation of reuniting FBI women, waiting to be bussed to a banquet, sitting together on the bus and talking over the awful American meal. He probably would have got drunk anyway, even on the pittance of wine they served, but with the food so plastic and inedible, there was nothing to cushion the alcohol. So he didn't remember much about the conversation. It had been about her. Her commitment. The communist world she and her husband had inhabited. The great hopes of the thirties and forties. The literary reviews. Tendency literature. Anti-fascist alliances. All the great absences of the present times, all the inexpressibles nobody wanted to talk about any more, and if somebody was there to talk about them they must have had an interest in them, mustn't they? But what sort of an interest, did he think to ask himself that?

The theorist of suspicion had an American friend who showed them round. The fraternities, the private clubs, the one every director of the CIA has been a member of. He didn't take them in. Maybe guests weren't admitted. Maybe he wasn't a member. All this exclusivity. Murky panelled walls and sporting photographs. A modest drink with lunch. Then he took them to the bookshops.

He picked up a book on the university and the intelligence community.

'You shouldn't read those sort of things,' said the American friend, 'they make you paranoid.'

It was written by the person who had given the welcoming address to the symposium. Without qualifications in Australian literature, indeed in any literature, he had welcomed them all the same. He bought a copy and read the account of Area Studies in the hotel before dinner. It explained how the growth of studies of particular regions and cultures had been invaluable for the intelligence services. The American friend was right, reading those sort of things made you paranoid. He wished he'd read it earlier.

'I get obsessed with images when reading your work and it is never the image that you directly suggest. This time I kept seeing Sydney harbour, all its ins and outs (which of course remains always visible to me from early days); so it either means that your work is full of youth or full of Sydney harbour or full of trips (boat trips!) of your (lucky) students coming to your classes—or maybe somehow a feeling you have given me that all your writing is a picture of some of Sydney now—the Sydney I did and did not know and which has changed with the years.'

When she came back it was no especially triumphant return. This was the country that had refused to publish her—'those cadaver publishers, those vampire corpses,' she wrote to him, 'it is terrible that everything has gone into their sickening maw.' This was the country that had banned one of her books. This was the country that had given her a prize and then withdrawn it on the grounds that she wasn't living there, that was the official story but the hand of the cold warriors was obvious. The money would have been useful. After the years of travelling and owning nothing she returned, still owning nothing. Later the biographers would write about her poverty, her lack of property, her absence of assets, as if this was a mark of failure. These were the years of greed, of acquisition, of 'lifestyle', and honest poverty was just a phrase to laugh at. She lived in a barn-like extension to a relative's house. It wasn't too different from how he lived himself, which was why he didn't especially remark it, except in those days he had a view of the harbour. But basically it was a big, rented space. 'Like a graduate student,' as some smart American poet he'd invited over sneered, flush with cultural interchange at the taxpayer's expense. But what else do you want, besides shelves for books, a bed, a chair, a table, a typewriter, what else in the end is the writer's life, who sees the beautiful view while writing, who needs the paintings and artefacts? We bring nothing into this world and assuredly we take nothing out of it.

'I am getting my place into some sort of order (it's only a sort of barn), for I want to ask Patrick to a restaurant near here and I can't do that without asking him to my barn; and his barn is so beautiful. (Whatever I do, I can't decorate mine with those painting masterpieces that cover his walls.) So I am now dithering as it seems, as usual.'

It was not important to her. The fetishism of materiality, the fetishism of place, neither was part of her world. He once asked her if she had ever revisited the house she grew up in.

'No,' she said aghast, 'why would I do that? Two of my brothers' marriages broke up there, why would I want to do that?'

Because it was on the map of literary pilgrimage, because it was on the shores of the harbour, a writer's house, he supposed. He had taken people to see it, the tourist track to the life of the mind, a touchstone of the social reality of fictional creation. But he felt abashed at her reaction, rebuked. And she was right. It was the books that mattered, the writing, not the writers' houses, not the bourgeois fetish of property but the writing that had tried to demolish that bourgeois rule.

He'd asked her once, 'You left the USA because of McCarthyism?'

'No, no,' she said, that deep voice, that peremptory dismissal, 'no, not at all, it didn't affect us.' Her husband had wanted to get back to Europe when the war ended, that was all. He was disappointed. In those days, at that time, in his innocence and ignorance, it had all seemed romantic, being harassed, being blacklisted, suffering martyrdom for the cause. The realities hadn't impinged then; well, you'd just keep on writing secure in the knowledge that history would vindicate you and redress all the wrongs. He didn't know, not having had the experience, how hard it would be to create in no context, how hard to write when all access to your readers was closed off, how hard to sustain a self image as a writer when nothing you wrote ever appeared, and when history's redress seemed an infinite distance away and far too late even if it ever were to come.

Nor did he know that his question wasn't the sort to elicit an answer. For those who had been on a blacklist, there was nothing but further exclusion to come by talking about it. It wasn't something you could afford to admit to. Nor indeed was it something you could ever point to. Who had actually seen the list? There was nothing finite. It was a system of absences and exclusions, all you could point to was not being in print, not being invited to contribute, not being mentioned in the criticism and histories and bibliographies, nothing palpable at all.

And while it all might have seemed remote, twenty-five years after, and a thing of history, anybody who had experienced it and still survived knew that it was something that never ended, that it was a strategy that had worked so well in the past that the secret state would never surrender it, that the list and the strategy was always there to be called on and activated and when the time came, which it did, to be expanded and put into operation again. Only this time there wouldn't be the public expression of it, no public hearings, no tribunals, none of the martyr-making apparatus, this time it would be silently and so much more effectively done. Anybody who had been through that once would know it would never go away, and that even the most casual inquiry about it was to be evaded.

So the conversation flagged a bit.

'When you went to Spain, was that for the Civil War?'

And again it was, 'No, no.'

They were in an Italian restaurant in a Sydney suburb. She had written: 'If you can really spare the time to come out here for a couple of hours, just let me know when—before lunch for drinks or in the afternoon for drinks. If for lunch, I suggest you come here just to see how I live (not in a palace but also not in a Grand Perpendicular Anonymous)—in a backyard; and then when we have had a drink or two, I suggest we go to a little restaurant near here, which I patronise because I do not want to make lunch here. I USED to, but ever since I tried to feed Judah and his sweet daughter Alice (violinist of high calibre) on an overcooked roast beef (put in the oven by Brother who loves overcooked ever since he spent his youth going round NSW and eating in small hotels in the heat) and this same overcooked roast which had looked so beautiful at the butcher's turned out to be most artistically tied up scraps—ever since then, I have taken people out to lunch to the little restaurant.'

The traffic surged past and it was hard to hear.

'No, no,' she said, 'it was before the war.' Her husband's partner had got the idea that with the republic there would be a lot of land going cheaply, all the aristocratic big landowners fleeing and selling out. 'It was one of his money-making schemes.'

'Did it work?'

'No, no.'

The low voice, the roaring traffic, he could hardly hear, only catch bits of it as she went on to tell him about living in Spain, writing a novel there, the cool dark room in the hot days. Then the war broke out and they left.

Again, in his world of unreality, it was disappointing. When later it all made sense, when later reality had caught up with him, then it was too late to talk to her, by then she had died. And something within him had died too. But perhaps it was only some of the young growth of naivety and now it had been shed and there was room for something else to grow. Yet if his expectations had been romantically unrealistic, hers had continued no less so.

'I think I saw a photograph of you (in the thick of it, the battle mentioned) in the paper yesterday, the *Morning Star,* caption 'Sydney rejects Thieu', you a heroic figure in the centre of police caps, banner, placards; they centred you because you photograph so well, no doubt.'

It hadn't been him, he was not one for demonstrations. They seemed all too much like the ritual of school games, stewards like prefects compelling attendance. And they just served to get your photograph on the files; he'd been to enough to realise that, special branch cameramen everywhere. For him as for her there were other sites of conflict, more elusive, more pervasive, sitting at the typewriter before the beautiful view, their own front line exactly where they were, with all the fear that it was an evasion, all the anxiety that they should engage more directly, the guilt that they didn't, their opposition much less palpable, much more encompassing, their own role so uneasily ambiguous. It was the ambiguities he found he could write about, as she had done. She responded to one of his stories, 'probably all writers do think sometimes "but what am I telling this and so much of it for? I am an informer!" and one hesitates to put in whatever one is writing—"I'm a fingerman." Well, it's a consideration, when you're writing of real events. "I'm an informer, too." What a shrinking! (However, like the bad poet in the Denis Diderot masterpiece, one goes on.) (*Le poète à Pondicherry*).'

One of the biographers came to Sydney and arranged to meet him. So we can talk about her. She had talked to her friends. Gained their trust. It had taken a while, they were a closed community, those old leftists. They didn't talk easily. But in the end they had talked to her.

He talked to her too. He was usually cautious, too. Not that he had much to talk about, there was a feeling, a sense of connection, but not much information, how many times had they met, after all, it had been an exchange of letters.

'Do you have them?' she asked. 'Can I see them?'

He still had them. At one point he had had a mass destruction of old papers, old letters, old postcards. He had kept only a handful of the material. He had kept her letters.

'Could I see them?'

He couldn't see any reason why not. He'd looked through them before she came. But he didn't want to leave her there with them, and he didn't want to sit wasting time while she read them, and he didn't want her to take them away. In the end he made photocopies for her.

She insisted they had dinner. And bring your wife. She was with her husband. It was a terrible evening. To begin with he got caught up in the afternoon, some sequence of things, and they arrived there about an hour late. The meal was chill, certainly the husband was. It was a not very good Chinese restaurant. Afterwards they hallucinated all night. 'I'm sure they poisoned us,' said his wife.

This was when he began to wonder if there was an agenda. Were these self-styled biographers continuing the investigation begun fifty years earlier? She and her husband were dead but did that mean the files were? Their names had been on so many secret service lists, they had lived in so many countries. Were the investigations never closed, agents for ever correlating names and places and visits, tracking down leftist friends and taking them out for dinner and poisoning them in bad restaurants?

She and her husband had been on file, but being on file was not an end in itself. Being on file was just the beginning. Then the harassment started, the blacklisting, the gossip to friends, the insinuations to publishers, the hints to editors. For twenty years she could not get her novels published. When she was published again it was all old materials, material she'd worked on during the blacklisted fifties, increasingly bleak, dark books, published out of their context, books without that earlier joy and energy. And now her books were back in view the biographers got to work. Was that all part of an agenda too, to present a negative picture, to resurrect all the secret service lies, all the innuendoes, all the sex-life, drinking, quarrelling scuttlebutt, and re-run it, now there was no-one alive to refute it, to divert attention from the novels, to distract and defame and discredit? Was that possible? It was all possible, all too possible.

But these are the things you never know. Sometimes you have suspicions, if you trust your intuitions you sniff out dangers, inauthenticities, but you never really know. She had written to him from New York: 'When I return (very shortly) I'll discuss some project with you . . . I have ideas in my head since I've been sitting around in enforced laziness (splendid to think I'm RIGHT to do it). One of them, the projects, is CASING THE JOINT—an autobiog. which should be fairly gay and in every way in fact the opp. of the things they are now forcing on me—collections of letters or "readers" and other nonsense of that sort. Just got very fed up with some academic juniors who wrote to me about woman's life and work or me in that role etc. And—spat! But no spit in CASING THE JOINT. Idea is that we spend the whole of our lives casing the joint we strangely find ourselves in and we have to, no Guide or Itinerary is any good . . .'

The first time they met was in England. She had written 'If you can fit me in, I should be delighted to have you here for lunch or dinner or a cocktail. Will invite a few friendly souls.'

If he could fit her in! Yet that was a truth she intuited even if he preferred not to. It was amazing he could fit anything in then, his whole life a maze of involvements and adventures and ambitions, recriminations and guilts and remorse, so caught up with his own sexuality, his own writing and rewriting, his own chaos of relationships and the writing of the moment, trying to be up to date, break with traditions without ever having known them, unaware of the blind alleys he was being led down. He dragged himself clear of the spires, the parks, the meadows, and went up to London.

They met at a restaurant in Soho. She had an old friend there, a typical Trotskyite turned small businessman, she characterised him. The friend responded that she was just an unrepentant Stalinist, and ordered lobster for them. It was a moment he always remembered, not the food, not the wine, not the place but the words, this friendly familiar skirmish that left both satisfied in having marked out their ground, their positions, the weight of history poised behind them with its lessons ready for whoever cared to learn. Afterwards she took him to meet another friend who was arranging medical aid for North Vietnam. There were depths of commitment here besides which he felt lightweight, unserious, a radical tradition refusing obliteration, challenging the current tendency of his own writing, calling to his political conscience. Later she described the characters in his first novel as 'except for the teller and the grand women, an objectionable lazy pleasure mad crew, reminding me of the children next door, madly riding their trikes and bikes and pedal-cars all day long, and shrieking unintelligibly (except, it means joy). I don't seem to like them? I didn't, but the dreary lotus land they live in sent some of its scented wind over to me, as you see.'

He could only agree.

He tried to deepen his concerns. Bit by bit he tried to learn the things she and her world had known. But for years the lotus land held him, becalmed there, and not reluctantly. They were safe waters. Once he left them things were never as easy again.

They met another time in Sydney but she had been ill that morning, angina, and did not feel able to go out. She offered drinks.

'Only if you want,' she said. 'I had a journalist come to interview me and I offered her a drink as one does out of politeness and she wrote me up as an alcoholic drinking gin and tonic at eleven in the morning.'

It had made her very angry.

She insisted he and his girlfriend should go out to lunch anyway, have it on her. She insisted on paying but she wouldn't come. She gave him a copy of one of her husband's books—'if you promise to read it'—and his girlfriend one of her cookbooks. 'All the things I like are bad for me,' she said, she couldn't cook them any more.

And the last meeting never happened. He'd spoken to her on the phone. He'd been asked to arrange an interview with her for a literary magazine. He approached her with some trepidation. They'd been out of touch for some time, she'd been out of Sydney, itinerant, he'd been in retreat. He'd once suggested publishing a book of interviews she'd given. She had been horrified. 'A dreadful idea,' she'd said, 'I regret them all.' Then he'd proposed a book of her occasional writings, and suggested she ask for a project grant to assemble it; someone had phoned him saying she had huge medical bills to pay after her heart attack in America. But she wouldn't have any of it. 'You get the grant,' she said. 'I don't need one,' he said. 'Nor do I.' This was when he still believed in interviews and government grants, before he'd reached her sane suspicions. So when he phoned her this last time he was dubious. And he wasn't doing the interview himself. But she agreed to do it.

'I'd like to see you again,' she said.

He felt bad he'd lost touch.

They arranged a time for him to visit. But when he phoned

again to confirm it he encountered relatives and they said it wasn't possible.

He regretted it. But it didn't matter. The meetings were never as easy as the letters. And the books were always there. Writers live in a world of writing, that's when they say what they mean to say, what they need to say, insofar as they ever can.

'Thanks—so glad you wrote. The last few days (that telepathic pre-post to which I am very subject) I have been thinking of you in these words: "I hope he didn't take it that I meant he wasn't to write: I like him to write."'